Murder by Proxy

MURDER BY PROXY

Anne Morice

ST. MARTIN'S
NEW YORK

Printed in Hong Kong

Library of Congress Catalog Card Number: 78–54106

First published in the United States of
America in 1978

ISBN: 0–312–55292–0

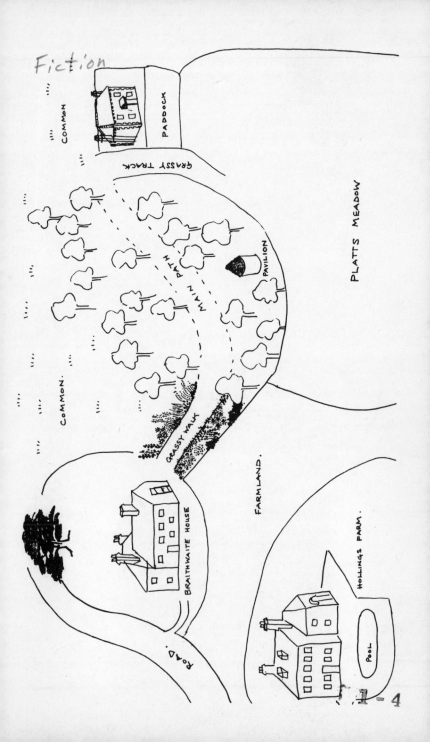

CHAPTER ONE

On the last Saturday of the run of *Post Haste,* a somewhat more leaden comedy than the title suggests, which had nevertheless managed to survive on Shaftesbury Avenue for almost six months, I had just returned to my dressing room after the curtain call when the stage door keeper rang through with the information that he had a young lady there, a Mrs Purveyance, asking if it would be all right to come up.

This being one of the less common names among my acquaintanceship, I concluded that its bearer had at last achieved her heart's desire and married the man of her dreams, whom she had been living with for the past five years and that she was none other than my old school friend, Anne Monk.

Congratulations were premature, however, and she cut them short by explaining that Harry was still bound by the chains of his legal marriage and that she had changed her name to his by deed poll, to spare their two-year-old daughter, Lizzie, from being shamed and humiliated at her play group.

"Besides," she went on, "it's even more essential now that we've got this new one coming. It's bound to be a boy and Harry is dead keen on his going to Eton and all those places."

"What makes you so certain this one is a boy?"

"Oh, don't you start, for God's sake, Tessa! I get enough of that from Cath, and it's really getting me down. Honestly, how would you like it if Robin had an ex-wife living practically on your doorstep?"

"A question I so often ask myself," I admitted.

Ignoring this flippancy, Anne continued almost without pausing for breath :

"And it's so unfair because they were separated ages before I met Harry, so no one can blame me for their marriage breaking up, though you'd never think so from the way Cath goes on. She's always telling me not to count my chickens before they're hatched, which is a most tasteless expression in the circumstances and she spends hours knitting up silly little pink woollen garments. It's partly to annoy and partly wishful thinking. She'll probably explode with jealousy when Harry and I have a son; but I can't help her troubles. And don't ask me how I know this one is a boy, I just do."

"How's Mary taking it ?"

"Oh, Mary's not quite so bad. Of course, she's madly jealous of anything which diverts a little more of her father's attention away from herself, but at the same time she'll be potty about the new baby when it's here. She's always creeping up to the pram and drooling over Lizzie when she thinks I'm not looking. Honestly, it's pathetic how mixed up that girl is."

Although not sharing Anne's confidence regarding the sex of her unborn child, it had not escaped me, the instant she entered the room, that it undoubtedly existed. She was such a frail, waif-like creature, so small boned and delicately made that even a four-months pregnancy had given her a top heavy look and the shadows under her large and melancholy brown eyes had deepened, as though the effort of carrying around this extra load had already brought her to the point of exhaustion.

There was nothing frail or wispy about her imagination, however. In fact, it was so powerful and wide-ranging that it sometimes seemed to devour not only most of her mental energy, but a lot of the physical kind as well. She was indolent to the point of lassitude, any form of exercise was hateful to her and she appeared incapable of undertaking the lightest domestic chore. Luckily for them both, Harry was a keen and accomplished cook and neither of them seemed to mind in the least how much dust and debris piled up in the house between the visits of Mrs Chalmers from the village, who toiled away for four hours every Monday and Thursday morning, sprucing it up again.

So, accepting that this vast imagination had no doubt been stimulated still further by her present interesting condition and, despite my first hand acquaintance with Harry's wife and daughter and the peculiar position they held in his household, I assumed that Anne had given a somewhat exaggerated account of their reactions, that it would be unwise to encourage her to further excesses, and attempted to cool things down by asking her how she had enjoyed the play.

"What play?" she asked in an abstracted voice.

"Well, damn it all! The one you've just sat through."

"Oh, that! Well, no, I haven't just sat through it, you see. There was no need to. We came to the first night and I thought you were marvellous and all that, but it's not exactly the kind of thing one could bear to see twice."

"Oh, I see. So you just dropped in for a bit of a chat? Well, that's nice! Is Harry with you?"

"No, he's at home, looking after Lizzie. I came up to see my father. He's been most terribly ill, did you know?"

"No, I didn't. I'm sorry. What's the matter with him?"

"No one seems to know. The doctor says it's only indigestion or something, but I'm positive it's much more serious. That's why I try to get up to spend an hour or two with him whenever I can, which isn't very often, actually."

"How rotten for you! But, listen, Anne, it's lovely to

see you, but I'm afraid I can't suggest going out for a drink or anything. We have two shows on Saturday and the curtain will be up again in half an hour. I'd scarcely have time to get my make-up off and on again."

"That's all right, I don't want to go out, not a bit. I came because I desperately wanted to talk to you in private, on your own ground, and this was the only way I could think of. I'm walking around with the most ghastly secret and if I don't unburden myself to someone I shall go raving mad."

Having known Anne since we were both the scourge of the lower third, the ghastly secrets she had shared with me in her time were too numerous to count; so I cordially invited her to go ahead, not with any true expectation of being harrowed, or indeed, more than mildly interested.

"I am absolutely certain that someone is trying to kill me," she announced, which was pretty run of the mill compared to most of her ghastly secrets over the years, although I am bound to admit that one or two moderately original twists did crop up in this one, as the tale unfolded.

"Is that so?" I asked, "you don't happen to know who?"

"No, it's too terrifying to think of. I can't bear to contemplate the idea of anyone hating me so much."

"Have you told Harry?"

"No, not a soul, except you."

"Why not? Do you suspect that he might be the one?"

"Of course not. Don't be an idiot, Tessa!"

"Then why haven't you told him?"

"Well, you know what Harry's like? He'd probably laugh himself into a fit; but he might take it seriously and go completely off the deep end."

"Which do you think is more likely?"

"How would I know? You can never be sure of anything with Harry. He's completely unpredictable most of the time and getting more so every day."

"What I'm driving at, Anne is this : do you accept the remote possibility that you've worked yourself up into a state over this, without any real foundation, or has something actually happened which he would be forced to take seriously? Either way, I should say it would be a good idea to relieve your feelings by telling him about it."

"I'd rather start by telling you and letting you judge for yourself."

"All right, so what exactly did happen?"

"There've been three things altogether. The first was when I got shut in the linen cupboard."

"How did that happen?" I asked, trying to sound solemn.

"I simply don't know. I went in to get some of Lizzie's clothes, which I'd left there to air. I left the door open because the bulb wasn't working, but while I had my back to the door someone shut it and there I was in the pitch dark. When I tried to push it open again it wouldn't budge. I'd been locked in."

"And then what?"

"I banged on the door and screamed blue murder, but I hadn't really much hope of being heard. I didn't think there was anyone in the house except me and Lizzie and what could she do, apart from going mad with fright too?"

"What time was this?"

"About ten in the morning. Harry was out shooting with Tom. It could have been ages before anyone discovered where I was. I could have died of suffocation or fright hours before."

"But you didn't, so presumably someone heard you?"

"Yes, Mary."

"What was Mary doing in the house at that time of day?"

"You may well ask, but as a matter of fact there was nothing particularly unusual about it. She spends most of her time hanging round our necks and it's worse than ever now she's left school and is completely at a loose end. I suppose she hadn't realised that Harry was out with a gun and wouldn't be back until the afternoon and she was hoping to run into him and get invited to lunch."

"But anyway she heard you and came to the rescue, so I suppose you should be grateful to her, for once?"

"She said she heard someone crying and she thought it must be Lizzie upstairs in her cot. So that was an opportunity not to be missed, you may be sure! Only when she sneaked up to the landing she realised what had happened and she opened the door."

"Just like that? The key was still there?"

"No, but she said it wasn't locked at all, just jammed a bit and if I'd pushed hard enough I could have got it open myself. She seemed to take the whole thing as rather a joke, but I can assure you it wasn't. There's no ventilation in there and the tank was boiling hot. I've never been more terrified in my life."

"Yes, horrid for you! What else, though? You said there'd been more than one attempt to finish you off?"

"The next one was my so-called gastro-enteritis. Dr. Bell insisted it was nothing worse and he said there was a lot of it going about, but he's one of those who, unless you actually cut your throat in his presence, always says there's a lot of it going about, and I'm bloody sure it was something much more sinister. The pain was excruciating and I was sick as a dog for twenty-four hours without stopping."

"From which you deduce that someone had been trying to poison you?"

"Well, wouldn't you? For one thing, it came on so suddenly, about three o'clock in the morning, when I woke up with these agonising stomach pains. I don't think ordinary gastro-enteritis would kick off as violently as that, do you? And I hadn't been feeling in the least queasy before. In fact, Harry cooked the most marvellous coq au vin for dinner and I ate quite a lot of it."

"Who else was at dinner?"

"Oh, Cath and Mary, wouldn't you know? You can absolutely depend on their turning up when there's something special on the menu. I think they must lean out of their windows and start sniffing at about seven o'clock."

"Anyone else?"

"Only Tom and some people called Nicholson, from Hollings Farm. They've got their daughter staying with them and they brought her as well. We'd invited your cousin, Toby, but he had to put us off at the last minute, which is why there happened to be enough for Cath and Mary. You know the Nicholsons?"

"Yes, but I'm not sure about Tom. He was the one in the shooting party, didn't you say? Have I met him?"

"You must have. He's Harry's great, tremendous buddy. At least he is now. Perhaps that's since your time, but he's another who's hardly ever off the premises these days. He's an estate agent, but in a very grand way, he wants us to know. Sells vast country mansions to pop stars and oil sheiks."

"So?"

"So nothing. He's a terrific snob and mad about money. I think that's the story of Tom."

"I wasn't referring to him, I was back on the main theme. I'm afraid I haven't been very constructive so far, but I was wondering if it had done you any good to unburden yourself?"

She looked up at me with a mournful expression, her

big dark eyes glistening with tears, as she answered slowly :

"I'm not sure, Tessa. Perhaps in a way, it has. One of the things I miss most is someone like yourself, someone of my own age to confide in. I was never much good at bottling things up, was I? On the other hand, talking about it and bringing it into the open at last has somehow made it more real and terrifying than ever. Can you understand that?"

"Up to a point."

"And anyway I haven't told you the whole of it yet."

"Oh dear, haven't you?" I asked, snatching a quick, sidelong squint at the travelling clock on my dressing table, "well, perhaps now you've started you'd better give me the lot, even if it does only make you feel worse than ever."

"The last time was only a week ago, my first day downstairs after being ill. Dr Bell made me stay in bed for two or three days, just in case it had had any bad effect on the baby; so I was feeling most terribly tottery when I did get up, and I fell downstairs."

"Well, hard cheese, Anne, but you can't seriously blame anyone else for that?"

"Yes, I can, because the reason I fell was that I stepped on one of Lizzie's rubber balls. Well, plastic, actually, but you know what I mean? They're hollow, very light and rather slippery."

"And the way Lizzie's toys are left scattered all over the house, it comes as no particular surprise that there should have been a plastic ball on the staircase."

"It ought to though, because she couldn't possibly have thrown it up as far as that, and if she'd chucked it down from above it would have bounced all the way to the bottom. There's just no way it could have lodged where it did, right underneath the third or fourth stair, unless someone had put it there deliberately."

"Were you much hurt?"

"No, only shaken and a bit grazed. Luckily, I tipped over backwards, so I just slithered a few yards, but I could easily have broken my neck and you can imagine how frightening it was? Honestly, Tessa, it's getting me down so badly that I'm beginning to feel quite suicidal."

"Oh, don't say that! If someone is really after you, there's no need to do their work for them. Your job is to fight back."

"I know, but I couldn't possibly manage it on my own. That's why I've come to you. Now, don't give me that haughty look, Tessa. I admit I've been devious, but I thought it would be better to begin by pretending that I just wanted to pour out my troubles and then slink away. I wanted to work up your interest and put you in the right mood to give me some practical help. You are interested, aren't you?"

"Oh, sure!"

"And you will help me?"

"I can't imagine how, but no doubt you've got all my instructions lined up in triplicate?"

"Yes, sort of. It was your cousin Toby who gave me the idea. We had dinner with him the other night and he told me the play was coming off soon and that you'd be going down to stay with him at Roakes for a few days."

"Yes, that's true. I go on Thursday and Robin hopes to join us for the weekend. What about it?"

"Well, I said I hoped to see something of you while you were there, and all that kind of stuff, to which he replied that you'd probably be too busy unearthing crimes to have much time for the social round, but that he'd do his best to head you off. I think he was only joking, actually, but honestly I nearly collapsed when he said it.

15

I managed to pull myself together enough to ask him what he meant and he told me that once or twice, in a murder case, you'd stuck your oar in and found things out. As a matter of fact, he said it was mainly a question of luck and the fact that Robin is a real life inspector from Scotland Yard, beavering away in the background and digging out all the hard evidence. But he did admit that you have this knack of chatting people up and worming your way into their confidence, and it sometimes ended with them giving you information they either didn't realise they had, or were madly trying to conceal, and that really made me think."

"Did it now?"

"It certainly did. As I told you, when he first began on it I was practically fainting. All I could think was that it would make a crime of some kind inevitable, that it had been pre-ordained in some way and that I'd been picked out in advance as the victim. It was as though I'd been told no matter how I tried to escape I would never be safe. But then, all at once, everything switched round and I began to look at it in another way. It struck me that perhaps someone up there was on my side, after all, and they were sending you, not to trigger off a crime, but to prevent one."

"Yes, I think I'd feel happier in that role."

"And, you see, Tessa, the way Toby described it, you're exactly what I need, the answer to a prayer. I could never possibly go to the police myself, how could I? But what I do need is someone like yourself, who knows all about us and the weird way we live, but is quite detached. You could stand outside it all, but watch what's going on, and then you could pass on to Robin anything you were able to find out and he could take the necessary steps, without anyone ever knowing that I'd had a hand in it."

"So you do believe that someone in the family is responsible?" I asked, ignoring the many flaws in this proposal.

"No, not necessarily. I mean, like I've told you, I simply can't face trying to fit a name or a personality to it. It would be too shattering. I just want it to stop."

"But if I were to find out for you, wouldn't it amount to the same thing?"

"No, that would be quite different. I shouldn't have to watch them and spy on them myself; I could leave all that to you. And you will do it, won't you, Tessa? At least, say you'll come over to the house sometimes and talk to everyone and get them to talk to you, that's all I'm asking."

"And what if it results in absolutely nothing? It's more than likely, you know."

She drooped her head in an attitude of infinite sorrow and resignation :

"Then I'll just have to think of something else, won't I? I can't endure much more of this; never knowing where the attack is going to come from next, or what form it will take. Do at least say you'll try! Please, Tessa!"

The last pathetic plea was punctuated by two smart raps on the door, followed by the shouted reminder that the curtain would be going up in ten minutes. It was no time for argument and I hustled her out of the room, airily promising to do my best.

The undertaking was given, I must confess, mainly to get rid of her, but all the same I was fully resolved to carry it out. As I have mentioned, there were one or two curious elements in her story and the principle one was that, although it was unlikely that any of the incidents she had described had genuinely been designed to cause her death, yet each, or still more all three in rapid succession, might well have brought on a miscarriage. I had come to the conclusion that it would be interesting to discover whether this had really been the intention and, if so, who had such an urgent motive for wishing the child to be still-born.

CHAPTER TWO

"Any news?" I enquired.

"Not that I recall. Certainly nothing that one of your ghoulish disposition would describe as sensational."

"Oh, that doesn't matter, Toby. Anything at all will do, no matter how trivial. I am just practising, you know. Chatting you up and worming my way into your confidence. I hear you had the Purveyances to dinner?"

Toby sighed: "I really believe that was my one and only bombshell. And now it turns out that you have already had the detailed account."

"Indeed I haven't. There is a lot more to hear. Why, for instance, did you break the habit of a lifetime and invite them here? You who never ask anyone to the house if it can possibly be avoided?"

"I suppose the answer is that it couldn't be avoided."

"Perhaps they invited themselves, like me and Tessa?" suggested Robin, who was also present, having taken a couple of hours off to drive me down to Roakes Common.

"No, not like that at all. You and Tessa are almost part of the furniture."

"That's not very flattering," I protested.

"Yes, it is. I am very deeply attached to my furniture. Every single piece is here because I chose it in the first place and it has proved its worth, in the second. That is a lot more than I can say for Harry Purveyance. In fact, I should not care if I never set eyes on him again, although Anne's grief stricken beauty has a certain poignancy. She has a lot to be grief stricken about, I understand."

"So the question remains: why did they come to dinner?"

"The answer may surprise you. As I've said, I seem to be immune to Harry's celebrated charm and I've certainly never regarded myself as being under the slightest obligation to invite him here. I rank as a comparative newcomer in these parts, whereas they tell me that his family has been here for three generations, at least. They used to own all the land as far as the eye could see, and right up to my azalea bed. Admittedly everything has now been sold off, to pay for his quaint indulgences, but he does not seem to feel that this has made any difference in our respective positions."

"Not quite everything, surely?"

"All but the woods between his own house and the cottage where he keeps his wife and daughter, plus about ten acres of meadow. It is less than a fifth of what there used to be. However, he still sees himself as the Seigneur of the neighbourhood, so the whole thing is rather a puzzle."

"What whole thing?"

"The way I've suddenly been taken up. I don't care for it at all. We used to meet about three times in a year and I had always assumed it was ample for both of us, but a few months ago the pattern changed, in a most drastic fashion. Invitations flooding in by every post and Mrs Parkes never off the telephone, explaining that I'd got pneumonia or gone to London. Even so, I couldn't hold out for ever. It would have looked rather pointed."

"So you finally succumbed and, having done so, felt it necessary to ask them back? Is that the answer?"

"In a very tightly packed nutshell. In fact, I had been bludgeoned into succumbing several times before I felt an overpowering obligation to return their hospitality, but the moment did come at last, so I invited them to dinner the following evening. You'd think that would have been safe enough, wouldn't you? Not at all. They accepted with such alacrity that I felt the ground literally slipping away from under my feet. And at any moment, I suppose, it will be their turn to invite me back again. They keep what used to be called a very good table, but the conversation is of the level which makes you want to slide underneath it, and I am not sure that I can take much more. Still, at least you can be an active piece of furniture while you're here, Tessa. You had better stay as close to the telephone as possible and intercept all calls. In fact, I think it might be best if you didn't leave the house at all."

"I can't absolutely guarantee that," I replied, "but for the next few days, at any rate, I promise only to leave it in order to call on Harry and Anne, which will be almost as good. I can create a diversion every time I see their hands straying to the telephone. Not that I'd worry too much, if I were you. They've got this wild crush on you at the moment, but I daresay it won't last. They'll drop you like a hot potato as soon as a new craze sets in. I've known plenty of people like that in my time."

"So have I," Robin said, giving me a peculiar look.

"We all have," Toby agreed, "but I doubt if it is as simple as that. I am not the only one to be getting the fulsome treatment. I've noticed several of my acquaintances huddled together at these beanos, being showered with champagne and compliments and they appeared to be just as bemused as I was. I have a nasty feeling there is something more sinister behind it."

I was reminded of this conversation the following morning, as I stood feasting my eyes, as the saying goes, on the ravishing, pastoral view from my bedroom window. It faced east, overlooking the garden and a vast stretch of open country beyond, a prospect much prized, as well as jealously protected by Toby and the half dozen or so nearby residents.

The wide belt of fields and woodland, from which the garden was invisibly separated by a ha-ha, sloped gently down towards the valley, but rose much more steeply on the farther side and on the highest point of all, hidden at this time of year by the trees, stood Braithwaite House, the home of Harry Purveyance.

In fact there were only two buildings to be seen in the whole panorama and, since each had a mellow, solid look about it, giving rise to the notion that it had been there almost as long as its surroundings, they enhanced rather than diminished its attractiveness.

The larger of the two was a brick and flint farmhouse, with a protecting flank of barns and outhouses, now discreetly converted into garages and other modern amenities, and was situated about halfway up the hill, on the left of the picture. It was still known as Hollings Farm, but now belonged to a middle-aged couple named Nicholson. They had acquired it about five years earlier, although all but three of the ninety acres it had once comprised had been sold to a neighbouring farmer, the same who had later extended his boundaries still further, to include most of the land formerly owned by the Purveyances.

The second and smaller house was perched on the very crest of the hill, almost in a direct line from where I stood, and was called Braithwaite Cottage. It still belonged to Harry, as did Platts Meadow, the ten acre field which sloped down in front of it. This land had now only one practical function, which was the provision of a permanent home for a superannuated donkey, although Harry's two remaining horses were also put out to grass there in the summer. I could not distinguish the donkey from that distance, but the horses were clearly visible, Harry's own black mare and a grey pony belonging to his daughter, Mary, and they too, decoratively grazing, occasionally lifting their heads as though to savour the warm summer morning, added an extra touch of magic to the view.

Although constructed in similar style and materials to Hollings Farm, the cottage was in fact quite modern, having been built between the wars by Harry's father, as a semi-detached dwelling for his cowman and gardener. Appropriately enough, it was now occupied by his semi-detached wife and daughter.

I remained for several minutes by the window, surveying the scene and recalling these facts to mind, and all at once, at some indefinable moment, it began to dawn on me that when they were all put together they provided a key to the riddle of Toby's new, unsought popularity and to precisely what it was that he had in common with some of his close neighbours. I did not consider that any of them had much to worry about, but unfortunately this was reckoning without Harry and his new friend, Tom.

CHAPTER THREE

In referring to my friend, Anne's powerful imagination, I may have omitted to mention that, although wide-ranging, it was not of the soaring variety which envisages all delightful things as possible, enabling her to wander through life, day-dreaming of huge wins on the pools, or of plunging in to rescue, singlehanded, a group of children from drowning. On the contrary, her images were invariably of the most macabre and catastrophic nature and it is safe to assume that any fictitious group of children would only have started to drown, and continued the process to the inexorable end, at the instant when she dived in amongst them. Inevitably, therefore, a fair slice of her imaginary life consisted in witnessing, failing to avert and blaming herself for ever after for a series of fatal accidents to her daughter, Lizzie.

It was more or less taken for granted that if Lizzie were to be left alone in a room for five minutes she would fall over and break her neck, fling herself on the fire and be burnt to death, or discover a bottle of poison under the sofa and drain it to the dregs.

She was equally convinced, apparently, that the wretched child would die of starvation unless every mouthful was ladled into her, having first been tasted and approved, with many a yum yum, by her mother, not to mention sundry dolls, teddy bears and other characters, live or inanimate, who happened to be present during a mealtime. Furthemore, it was an accepted truth that Lizzie would develop deep rooted paranoic tendencies if crossed or corrected in any particular and, however tired, would be incapable of closing her eyes unless lulled, soothed and joggled to sleep for at least half an hour at the start of any rest period. In the last instance all onlookers were assigned the passive role of maintaining a strict, unbroken silence until the object had been achieved.

So I was not seriously put out to arrive at Braithwaite House soon after six the following evening, Anne having implored me to come early, and to be told that she was incommunicado in the night nursery.

The news was given to me by Catherine Purveyance, who, as I entered from the garden, was sitting bolt upright in a high backed chair in a corner of the drawing room, in what struck me as a curiously attentive attitude for one who seemingly had nothing more absorbing on her mind than the bundle of pink knitting spread on her lap, and a television set, which had the picture switched on, but not the sound.

Cath, at this time, was aged about forty, though still pretty in a rather faded, pre-Raphaelite style, having a pale oval face, abundant soft, fine hair, very dowdily set, and an habitually martyred expression. Her clothes on this, as on every occasion for as long as I could remember, were neat, colourless and totally unremarkable. In fact, I had sometimes suspected her of thrusting each newly bought garment straight into an oak chest, in its original wrappings, and of leaving it there for a specified number of years; for I could not recall ever seeing her in anything which did not look at once brand new and a decade out of date.

The french windows from the garden opened into what had originally been the main hall, but which had recently been converted by Harry, in a rather clever and attractive fashion, into more up to date living quarters, combining a sitting room and kitchen.

The original stone fireplace and oak staircase still remained, but beyond them, and framing one third of the total space, was a wide archway, flanked on each side by waist high, pale oak shelves, with cupboards and drawers below, which bisected the room to within two or three feet of the side walls, the extreme edges being panelled up to the ceiling. The only points in the larger room from which the kitchen was invisible were beside the fireplace, where the view was blocked by the staircase, and in the opposite corner, where Cath was now seated.

She was among the sternest of Anne's critics and on this occasion launched into an impassioned attack on her misguided child-rearing methods before I even had both feet over the threshhold, a feat which was not made easier to accomplish, in any case, by a pile of wooden bricks having been left strewn across the doorway. The need to unburden herself was evidently so urgent that she got up at once and, taking my arm, propelled me outside again towards a wooden seat on the lawn, talking nineteen to the dozen as she went.

I felt slightly irritated by this high handed behaviour, but Cath was celebrated for her tactlessness, and a still more daunting characteristic was a kind of simmering, pent up hysteria, always struggling to burst out and not infrequently doing so, and I resigned myself to listening to a good ten minute, non-stop abuse of my old friend.

"It's a good thing you've come," she said, when the tirade had got well into its stride, "perhaps you can knock some sense into her, for I assure you that I have failed completely. If you ask me, she's simply ruining that poor child, turning her into a proper little monkey and making life a misery for everyone else as well, by pandering to her in this ridiculous way. Imagine sitting up there in the dark every evening, sometimes for hours on end, shooshing a great healthy girl of two until she goes to sleep! I ask you, Tessa! And what will happen when she has two of them to cope with simply beats me. You're not getting cold, are you? At least, it's quiet and peaceful out here. Sometimes the chaos and untidiness of that house gets on my nerves so badly that I could scream."

It was tempting to suggest that she would have been more usefully employed in tidying some of it up than in complaining about it, but Anne had impressed upon me that I was to be the sweet and patient listener, with a sympathetic ear always at the ready for whatever revelations might come its way, so I let the last remark pass, saying in a sweet and patient tone :

"But Cath, won't the problem solve itself when there are two of them? She simply won't be able to give them both the same attention as Lizzie gets now. It would be a physical impossibility."

" You're too optimistic, my dear. If you ask me, she'll be twice as bad and the house will be even more neglected than it is already. Worse than ever, if the new one should happen to be a boy, as she never stops telling us."

"Yes, I noticed she seemed pretty confident on that score. I wonder why?"

"If you ask me, it's just a lot of rubbish. Something about the way she's carrying it, I gather. That's another thing you might work on. The disappointment is likely to send her crazy, if it does turn out to be a girl, which is more than likely, as I do my best to explain to her. After all, Harry has two daughters already, so I imagine the chances are heavily in favour of a third. That is, if . . ."

"If what?"

"Oh, nothing, dear, nothing whatever. Just some stray remark of Tom's which came into my head; but one shouldn't pay attention to such things. And perhaps you shouldn't pay too much attention to me, either. I worry about them all too much, that's my trouble."

"All the same, you must have meant something, Cath. Were you about to say that if Anne goes on like this, working herself into such a frenzy of anxiety about Lizzie and everything else, she's liable to have a miscarriage and lose the baby altogether?"

"Good gracious, no; such an idea never entered my head," she replied, with such a genuinely startled look that I had no option but to believe her and mentally chided myself for having revealed my hand so early in the game.

"Then what did you mean?"

"Now, do stop pestering me, Tessa, there's a good girl! If you ask me, you're too inquisitive for your own good and you know I'm the last one to repeat malicious gossip, even if I believed it. Now, let's hear about yourself! How is it that you can get away from London on a weekday? No play going on at the moment?"

Even when she was not trying, and in this instance I was prepared to give her the benefit of a small doubt, Cath had an infallible talent for picking out the tender spot and jabbing away at it and, by the time she had finished commiserating on my lack of employment, with several passing references to the chanciness of my chosen profession, among other consolatory remarks of that nature, I was deeply relieved to hear her admit that perhaps it was turning rather chilly and we should be better off indoors.

"Such a pity this side of the garden gets so little of the afternoon sun," she sighed, as we walked back to the house. "That's one thing I can say for my tiny cottage; we get such beautiful sunsets. It's quite a joy to sit by my window of an evening just drinking it in. I get quite annoyed with poor Mary sometimes, when she comes

29

bursting in and spoils it all by switching on the light. But there you are, we can't all have the same tastes and appreciations. But still, you haven't come here to waste your time talking to me, and there's always the chance that Anne will have decided to join us by now."

As it happened, she had not, but I was spared another confidential session with Cath because Harry and his friend, Tom, were in the kitchen.

They were seated at the table, which was covered with what appeared from the other side of the archway to be architects' plans and were so engrossed in them that they did not notice us until Cath called out. Whereupon Harry got up hastily and came through to greet me, with typically exuberant hugs and kisses, while Tom furtively scuffled the papers together and folded them away in a brief-case.

The curious thing was that they had given a strong indication of having been engaged in their business for some considerable time and it set me wondering whether Cath had had some motive, other than the innocent desire to denigrate Anne, for hustling me out of the way so unceremoniously.

"And what have you two conspirators been up to?" she now enquired in the arch and bantering tone she reserved for Harry and which, strangely enough, never appeared to grate on his nerves, although Anne winced perceptibly every time she heard it.

However, this Harry was a man of contradictions, from start to finish. Work shy, yet bursting with vitality, clinging like a limpet to his ancestral home, with all its money draining inconveniences and not seeming to care how shabby and neglected it became; curiously detached and indifferent to the feelings of those closest to him, yet jealously protective of them as well, and possessing, in

30

spite of it all, a charm which I truly believed to be founded on a genuinely kind and generous nature.

Endowed at birth with looks, brains and money, he had set about at an early age to squander the lot. Having outstripped most of his contemporaries at school and university, he had been tipped for a scintillating diplomatic career, but had degenerated, through laziness and self-indulgence, into a somewhat fond and foolish, unmistakably overweight and uxorious middle-aged man, a landowner bereft of his land and a scholar with no higher ambition than to gratify every passing whim.

During one fruitful period, before his marriage, he had acquired a modest reputation from translating Russian drama and poetry; in the latter years, although always ostensibly at work on some oeuvre of enormous value to the civilised world, his output had been mainly confined to reviewing other people's efforts in that direction.

Another contradiction was that, while so good-humoured and easy going himself, he seemed to be irresistibly attracted to women who possessed neither of these qualities, for both Cath and Anne existed on a high plane of nervous tension. Admittedly, it took different forms and it was a great mystery to some of his friends that a man who so patently adored Anne could have started out by loving Cath. Beneath their superficial differences, however, I had noticed a number of traits in common, including a profound indolence and marked lack of humour. Certainly, in my opinion, he once had loved Cath and probably still retained strong feelings of affection for her, since it was he, by all accounts, who had prevailed on her to remain, as near as makes no difference, under his roof when their marriage broke up and who encouraged her to regard herself as still part of the family. Moreover, he was also clearly devoted to his elder daughter, Mary, who closely resembled her mother in all too many respects.

Still another conflicting element in his character was typified, in my view, by his friendship with Tom, who now, having tucked the papers away and placed the brief-case underneath his coat, cap and string gloves, which were neatly arranged on a chair by the back door, came through from the kitchen to join us.

I had indeed met him before, as I had instantly realised, although he was either unaware of this, or affected to be and cocked a very quizzical eyebrow when Harry introduced me as Tessa Price, alias Crichton. He then listened with polite indifference while it was explained to him that these were my married and stage names, signifying with everything except words that he was equally unfamiliar with both and fully expected to remain so. None of this did anything to modify my previous impression, that he was a posturing ass and probably as bent as a paper clip too.

However shabby in character, though, this was in no way reflected in his appearance, for he was good looking, in an ultra smooth, well groomed fashion, about the same age as Harry, but approximately half his weight and wearing the most immaculate tweed suit and suede ankle boots. Perhaps the intention was to portray the very essence of prosperous country gentlemanliness, but in my prejudiced view the effect was more like a model dressed up to pose as such.

Cath, who had mentally detached herself as soon as she ceased to command attention, now moved away to stand beside one of the room dividing ledges, where she stood like one transfixed, gazing in rapture at the kitchen.

"I can never get over how beautiful and attractive you've made it," she said, turning back to Harry and

32

interrupting him in mid-sentence and, for once, she did not exaggerate.

It really was a triumph of a kitchen, containing every domestic device known to man, all laid out and slotted together with a precision worthy of an operations room at Cape Canavarel, but cosy too, with a carpeted floor and bowls of fruit and flowers and bright coloured cushions to detract from the clinical effect. It was also very tidy, in marked contrast to our side of the barrier, a condition made easier to achieve and maintain, no doubt, by its being out of bounds to Lizzie, lest she might take the notion to climb on top of the Aga, or curl up inside the refrigerator.

"I turn green with envy every time I see it, I'm ashamed to tell you," Cath said with a plucky smile. "Such a contrast to that little cubby hole I have to work in . . ."

There was a faint clatter of heels on the staircase and she spun round sharply. Harry also looked up at the sound and his expression changed instantly from benign amusement to something more like besotted affection.

Anne was moving very slowly down the polished oak staircase, supporting herself with one hand on the broad, flat bannister rail, but when she came within a few steps of the bottom Harry moved forward and stood at the foot of the stairs, with arms outstretched, and she gave a little spring forward, to be caught, lifted off her feet and swung round like an adored and precious child, making it wincing time for Cath, who turned her back on the scene and quickly became absorbed in her bundle of pink knitting.

"And what is Cath turning green with envy about now?" Anne asked, still wearing her smug, little-girl smile.

"Only our beautiful new kitchen, my dearest; but

we're going to see that she gets one just like it, only a tiny, tiddly bit smaller, aren't we, my love? And Mary shall have her own little car to dash about in and be as happy as the day is long. Isn't that right, Tom?"

Neither of them answered him and Cath also ignored the questions, apparently intent on counting the stitches on her needle and casting thoughtful looks at the pattern book.

"Is baby Lizzie asleep?" Harry asked, after a brief pause.

"All but. My God, I thought she'd never quieten down to-night, but we're okay now, touch wood. Hallo, Tessa love, I didn't see you. Have you been here long?"

"No, not very."

"That's good because I can see that no one's given you a drink yet. And they can get one for me as well, while they're at it. My God, I need it. Over an hour I've been up there to-night."

"And you shall have one, my pet, right away. Tom will see to it while I run upstairs and say goodnight to Lizzo."

"Don't you dare!" Anne protested with a scream of exasperation, "not unless you want me to kill you. She was almost asleep when I left and if you get her wound up again we'll have no peace the whole evening."

Tom, who had been looking increasingly out of his element during these domestic high jinks, now entered the fray with a poor attempt at jocularity:

"Sorry, chaps, but I must be on my way. The social whirl calls, don't you know."

"I thought you were staying for dinner?" Harry said, looking put out.

"Very good of you, old boy, and nothing I'd like better, but I'm afraid it's not on to-night."

"Not even time for a drink before you go?"

"No; sorry and all that, but the Crossley-Jones are giving one of their fiestas and I have to pour myself into the old bib and tucker."

"I'll come out to the car with you," Harry told him, "there are a couple of points I need to clear up before we launch the boat. Be a lamb, Tessa love, and give yourself a drink, and the girls too, will you?"

They went out together by the back door from the kitchen, talking in undertones, and then Cath said:

"Crossley-Jones? Who on earth would they be?"

"New people is who they would be," Anne replied, collapsing on the sofa and holding out a languid hand for her gin and tonic, "Tom conned them into buying the Denbys' old wreck of a house. Stinking rich and trying desperately to get in with all the locals. They invited me and Harry to one of their parties, and I must say we were dying to go, but we had to put them off at the last minute because we couldn't get Mrs Chalmers to baby-sit. Thanks awfully, Tessa."

"Want a drink, Cath?"

"No thank you, dear, nothing for me. You can always rely on Mary and me for baby sitting; you know that, Anne?"

"Yes, thank you, I do know. And where is Mary, by the way? Don't tell me she has something else to do to-night?"

"Oh, she'll be along presently. She had to shut the hens in and feed the dogs, and one or two other little jobs, but I expect she'll be here soon."

"Yes, I'm sure she will."

"Harry invited us, you know, dear. We shouldn't dream of imposing on you otherwise. He happened to catch me in the garden when he came back from his ride this afternoon and he was most insistent about it. He said he had a very special . . ."

35

"Dish in the oven? I bet he did and I just hope Mary comes soon, so that he can take it out of the oven, because I'm famished."

"Well no, that isn't quite accurate. What he actually said was that he had something very special to tell us to-night. But still, I daresay that was before . . ."

"Before what? You're a great mistress of the unfinished sentence to-night, Cath. Before what?"

"Nothing, dear. It has no importance."

"It has to me. Before what?"

"I think what Cath means," I said, knocking back my drink and setting the glass down on the tray, "is that Harry gave out this news before he'd heard that I'd be here. No one has to worry, though. I'm not staying for dinner."

"Oh yes, you are : Harry won't mind in the least your hearing whatever it is he's going to tell us. Cath makes it sound very heavy and mysterious, but I expect it will only turn out to be a new rose bed he's planning or something. Anyway, I invited you."

"Only for a drink, which I've now had, and Toby's expecting me back for dinner. I did tell you that, Anne."

This was true, as it happened, and I suspected her of being perfectly aware of it and of trying to get me to stay principally to annoy Cath. However, there are limits to the obligations of friendship and I said firmly :

"I'm only waiting for Harry to come back, so that I can say goodbye and then I'm off."

A moment later he did so and Anne called out in her most petulant voice :

"Tessa is threatening to leave now, Harry. Do tell her she mustn't."

I was never to know how he would have responded to this because, before he had a chance to speak, the garden door was wrenched open and Mary burst in, tripping

36

over some of the wooden bricks and throwing her hands high in the air, with fingers outstretched.

Although now seventeen, she was still the same overgrown lump of a girl, whose natural prettiness was almost totally obscured by sloppy, unkempt clothes and hair. The near fall and last-second recovery produced an extra impetus and, deliberately exaggerating this, she swayed forward and flung herself on Harry, practically knocking him to the ground.

"Awfully sorry, Daddy darling," she said when they had both righted themselves, "but I see Lizzie's been at it again. I'm sure she means to kill Big Sister one of these days. And don't let me touch you, whatever happens. My hands are absolutely filthy."

"Couldn't you have washed them?" Anne asked, "you're not so late that two more minutes would have made any difference."

"You really should have, you know, darling," Cath said, adding in her prim voice, "before you came out."

"I know and I'm awfully sorry, but I'd shut the dogs in before I realised what a state they were in and the dogs would have raised the roof if I'd gone back. Never mind, I'll just dash upstairs to the bathroom and get the worst of it off," Mary shouted, now hurling herself at the staircase.

"You may as well get it all off, while you're at it," Harry remarked good humouredly and simultaneously there came a high pitched squeal from Anne :

"Couldn't you use the downstairs one, for God's sake? Cath, tell her to use the downstairs one!"

"Too late, I fear," Cath replied, smiling complacently at her knitting.

"Then for God's sake, don't pull the plug!" Anne yelled after Mary, who was now halfway up the stairs, "I'll see to it later."

Cath dropped her knitting on to her lap, the better to lean forward and express her deep concern :

"Now, really, my dear, isn't that going a bit far? I do realise it's not for me to interfere, but if you ask me you'll be the one to suffer in the end from this ridiculous over-cosseting. You'll never have a moment's peace unless you can train Lizzie to sleep through normal household sounds. The poor little soul will grow up to be nothing but a nuisance to herself and everyone else and she won't thank you for it in the end. Aren't I right, Harry?"

"You may well be, my darling, but we all have to follow our own line, you know. Can't do more, can we? Are you really leaving us, Tessa? You do realise you'll be missing the steak and kidney pud. of a lifetime?"

"Oh, that's too bad, but I must go, all the same. I promised Toby," I said, moving with moderate speed towards the garden door and then pausing to kick aside some of the wooden bricks, "bye, Cath."

"Goodbye, my dear. My regards to your cousin."

"I'll call you to-morrow, Anne. Maybe you could bring Lizzie over to tea one . . ."

With my hand on the doorknob, I broke off in mid-flow because from upstairs, faintly at first, but turning the volume up as she got into her stride, came Lizzie's plaintive wail, mingled a few seconds later with bleats from Mary :

"I'm most awfully sorry, Anne, but it wasn't my fault, honestly. All I did was just peep in and . . ."

They were all watching her as she came tumbling down the stairs, so I flapped my hand in a general fare-well, let myself out and gently closed the door behind me.

CHAPTER FOUR

"So the plot is thicker than I gave her credit for," I remarked during dinner, which, by a strange coincidence, featured a very superior steak and kidney pudding from the hand of Mrs Parkes, "and it cannot be called an easy assignment."

"You will triumph in the end, I daresay. Where does the difficulty lie?"

"Too many complications and cross currents. Apart from a whole battery of hints and innuendos, Anne believes that either Cath or Mary wishes to kill her, in which she may well be correct. She would certainly take pleasure in killing both of them and no one could blame her. If Harry were to kill all three of them I am sure that any reasonable judge would give him a minimal sentence, and Mary mentioned in passing that her own life was being threatened by Lizzie. It is quite a lot to have emerged in less than an hour and, just to round it off, I might be tempted to take up the hatchet myself."

"Against whom?"

"Harry's friend, Tom."

"Oh, but why? He's quite harmless, surely? Rather agreeably obsequious, I've always found."

"That must be in case one of your plays should hit the jackpot and put you in the market for a heavily timbered residence, with double gold plated sauna. He doesn't bother to be obsequious to me, I must tell you. Went out of his way to let me know he'd never heard of me and never expected to."

"I know," Toby admitted, "I am afraid that is all too

often the other side of the obsequious coin. It's understandable; people have to level the score somehow. I
wonder where the chip comes from on that smartly clad
shoulder?"

"Oh, plenty of old, unforgotten snubs, I should say;
and anyone who goes about dressed up as an advertise-
ment for Remy Martin has to be a phoney. However, I'll
settle his hash in due course. There's a lot of ground to
be covered first."

"It sounds like it and I am afraid I can only offer you
one tiny consolation."

"Anything, however small, will be welcome, Toby."

"You can at least eliminate Harry from your list of
potential murderers. Although you and I consider that he
would be perfectly justified in killing off all those three
females, either singly or at a mass slaughter, I know from
my own observation that he has no desire to do any such
thing. He goes to the most extraordinary lengths to keep
his little harem together, virtually under one roof."

"Yes, I know, isn't it weird? He's like one of those
lovely old fashioned Indian Princes, adding one wife
after another, complete with offspring, to the great big
happy family. I suppose he'd be bored stiff if he had to
manage with just one woman in his life, but Anne told
me once that it all came from his being an only child and
a very late one, at that. His parents hadn't particularly
wanted him and his youth was blighted by the constant
feeling of being lonely and excluded. That's what
brought on this obsession about gathering a family of his
own around him and why he's so terrified of any of them
breaking loose."

"I should have thought Anne could persuade him to
allow a couple of them to break loose, now that she's providing him with a complete little new family."

"I doubt if they'd consent to go, and unfortunately

she's not in a very strong position for that kind of persuading. She is not his legal wife, you know. That honour still belongs to Cath, who probably deludes herself that one of these days it will all come right for her and she'll be back in the four-poster. I wouldn't rate her chances very highly."

"Nor me, although I still think Anne is sadly misguided to tolerate the present situation."

"I agree, Toby, but there it is. No accounting for the human heart, as they say, and she's wild about that Harry. Besides, she's in too deep to draw back now. In the early days, before Lizzie was born and when she was a relatively free agent, I once put it to her that she'd do better to leave him, since he wasn't prepared to give up anything for her sake, and find herself some more suitable partner in life, and what do you think her answer was to that?"

"Something moronic, I daresay."

"No, it was rather shrewd, in fact. She said it would never work because, even if she did find someone she could be happy with, Harry would get round him in no time to move in with Anne and himself, so that they could all be cosy together, with lots of hot dinners and one more member to add to the family. There may be something in it."

Before Toby could comment the telephone rang and, moved to compassion by his hunted look, I left my dinner to go out to the hall and answer it.

"You can stop cowering," I told him, returning to my seat some minutes later, "it was only the Nicholsons and it's me they're after, not you. More marital problems, I regret to say."

"With the Nicholsons? I don't believe it! And what possible business could it be of yours?"

"No, not the Nicholsons in that sense. Not Mr and

Mrs, I mean. It's their daughter, Jane. Did you know that she'd separated from her husband and come back to live with Mummie and Daddy?"

"Yes."

"Well, they're pretty fed up about it, I can tell you. However, after mooning about and getting under their feet for a week or two, she has now upped and got herself a job in Storhampton."

"That must be some relief?"

"Not altogether. For one thing, it made it clear to them that she regards the present arrangement as somewhat more permanent than they had been hoping for, and secondly they don't at all approve of the job itself."

"Why not? Don't tell me she has become a traffic warden? They're about the only people I ever see actually working in Storhampton."

"No, she's with an estate agency. Need I say more?"

"Your friend, Tom? Well, there's nothing wrong with that, is there? If she felt the urge to work in an estate agency, she could hardly have picked a plushier one."

"Unfortunately, it doesn't end there. The assistant-boss relationship has rapidly deepened into something a good deal warmer. Tom has taken to calling for her of an evening and escorting her to all the smart Storhampton night spots, and that is really bugging them."

"Aching snobs, of course."

"Oh, I agree, but they don't object solely on those grounds. As Mrs Nicholson pointed out, he must be almost twice her age and furthermore the chances of getting her restored to her husband are seriously diminished so long as Tom is dancing attendance day and night."

"Very frustrating for them, I do see that, but what are you supposed to do about it?"

"I am afraid the poor woman lives in a dream world.

Having heard that I was staying here, it flashed into her mind with the speed of lightning that if only Jane were to be provided with companionship among her own generation, and . . . well, she didn't quite add class, but it was touch and go, it would break the spell and in no time at all she would begin to see Tom the bumptious brute he is, etcetera. To-morrow being Saturday, I am invited to join the morning cocktail session round the swimming pool and get stuck into this programme without delay. A sillier idea, I need hardly say, never crossed anyone's mind, but I intend to go, just the same. If Robin gets down in time, he is sure to want to spend the day playing golf and you will have to answer the telephone yourself, for once. I may as well add that, if invited to stay for lunch, I may easily do so."

"Since you have taken such a dislike to poor Tom and admit the plan is doomed to failure, I wonder you should allow yourself to become embroiled?"

"Well, it's what Robin calls all grist to the mill, isn't it? Besides, one can't be swayed by personal prejudice in matters of this kind. Tom might easily provide a key to some of the enigmas of Braithwaite House. He and Harry are clearly involved in some secret and probably shady enterprise, so it might be worth while cultivating him, with a view to finding out a little more about that. Anyway, I've told Mrs Nicholson I'll go."

"And where was Jane while this conversation was taking place? Out with the dreaded Tom, presumably?"

"Yes, and that's the *bonne bouche* I've been saving for you."

"But I understood you to say it had become a regular thing?"

"Quite so, but there's something special about this evening. You see, just before I left the Purveyances, Harry invited Tom to stay on for dinner, but he refused.

43

He couldn't even stop for a drink. His excuse was that he'd been invited to a very posh party and had to go home and change. So that's curious, don't you think? Why couldn't he have just explained that he was going out with his girl?"

"Well, let's say that he is a relentless show-off and was hoping to impress you all?"

"You may be right, but, after all, Jane is very dishy in her way and the Nicholsons are pretty loaded, so there's a name worth dropping too. No, I have a slightly different theory."

"And a far more sinister one, no doubt?"

"The way I see it is that, for some reason as yet undisclosed, he is madly anxious not to offend Harry. Therefore, when he is invited to dinner he does not consider it prudent to turn it down just for some casual date which could easily be broken or postponed. He has to go and invent some formal occasion which it would be quite impossible to get out of at the last minute. And you see where that leads us, don't you?"

"No, not in the least."

"If he is so dead keen not to offend Harry, doesn't it follow that Harry has some hold over him? Whether it has any bearing on Anne's troubles or not, it could do no harm to find out what it is."

"As you bob up and down in the swimming pool to-morrow?"

"Well, it's a start, isn't it? And one has to start somewhere. How fortunate that I brought an extra suitcase with all my beach gear!"

CHAPTER FIVE

My friendship with Jane Nicholson did not date from our schooldays, for her parents had not arrived in the neighbourhood until these were over, although I doubt if it would have made much difference, since it was clear from our first meeting that we were not to be compatible. Some people might consider that I had the better excuse for my antagonism, for there was no denying that, in addition to being rich, Jane was a great beauty; not, in my opinion, a patch on Anne, whose looks had a haunting, ethereal quality which to many people made them irresistible, but easily outclassing most of our contemporaries. On the other hand, it had been her contention throughout her teens that she would knock Elizabeth Taylor reeling back on the ropes once she got to Hollywood, which could only be a matter of time, and had not forsaken this dream until turned down by no less than three drama schools, so my head was bloody but unbowed.

Not that there was any overt hostility and we had always kept up a pretence of friendliness. She had been at my wedding and I went to hers and when, after the latter, she moved to London, we had lunched together once or twice a year. There had even been a period when Robin and I were roped in to make up a foursome, as they liked to call it, with Jane and her husband, a portly, facetious, true blue Tory, aged twenty-four, by the name of Charles Ewart. But since they both appeared to be under the impression that one medium hot dinner from the deep freeze entitled them to free seats for practically

45

every show in London, not to mention waiving of parking fines, this game had rapidly fizzled out.

On the whole, I preferred her parents, a dull and devoted couple, but both possessing charm in their different ways. Mrs Nicholson was a shy, sad faced woman who, had she gone about wearing a wimple or even a Balaclava helmet, would have looked very much like a model for an early Flemish painting, for she had round, rather staring eyes, a small round mouth and a long straight nose in between. She was sensible not to wear either headgear, however, for her best feature was her hair, soft and curly and a beautiful golden red. The colour was beginning to fade now, but it was still an attribute which many women half her age would have coveted.

Mr Nicholson was a complete contrast, in both looks and personality, but might also be described in pictorial terms, for he was like a walking embodiment of The Laughing Cavalier, with a large red jolly face and heavy black moustache. He was reputed to be a financial wizard, a connoisseur of Georgian silver and expert cultivator of roses, but was singularly ill informed on every other subject under the sun and his contribution to the social scene was virtually confined to bursts of ill-timed and uproarious laughter. According to Toby, this was purely a defence mechanism, designed to conceal the fact that he rarely had the remotest idea what people were talking about and rather hoped not to find out.

Since Robin had taken the car to the golf course and Toby pretended to be spending the morning at work on his current dramatic opus, I was obliged to go on foot to Hollings Farm. It was no great distance, but the latter part of the journey consisted of a steep climb up from the valley, followed by a shorter and more gradual slope through the terraced garden to a low yew hedge, which

46

enclosed the swimming pool and paved courtyard. On reaching this point I paused for a moment or two, getting my breath back and surveying the scene within.

Neither of the senior Nicholsons were present, but there were four other people disposed around the pool, all in bathing suits. On my side of it and with their backs to me were Jane and two unknown youths, while Tom, natty as ever, and tanned to a stylish nut brown, was on the far side, nearest the house. Curiously enough, he appeared to be taking no interest whatever in the other three and was engrossed in a newspaper; whereas the two boys, who could have been aged anywhere between sixteen and twenty, and whom I later discovered to be a Nicholson nephew and the nephew's friend, out from school for the day, were sitting with their knees hunched up, gazing at Jane in rapturous admiration, which I am bound to say was not misplaced.

Marriage, or possibly the severance of it, had certainly added an extra bloom and she was even more dazzling than when I had last seen her; straight and with flawless skin and the breathtaking red gold hair, which she had inherited from her mother, curling like a baby's all over her head and into the nape of her luscious creamy neck.

There was a certain amount of teasing going on and, as I stood watching, Jane advanced several times to the edge of the pool, raised her arms high above her head, balancing on tiptoe as though about to dive in and then, as the world around her held its breath, either lost her nerve or pretended to and, dropping her arms, turned round to exchange giggles and repartee with her two admirers.

On the third repetition of this small charade Mr and Mrs Nicholson emerged from the house, one pushing a trolley and the other carrying cushions and a green parasol, whereupon the tableau round the pool sprang

47

into life. Tom dropped his newspaper and jumped up to offer assistance, Jane overbalanced and hit the water with a smack which was painful to the ear, and the two boys also scrambled up and hurled themselves into the pool. I walked sedately through the gap in the hedge and joined the party.

From that moment on, the entire enterprise descended into pure fiasco because by the time I came out of the changing pavilion, wearing my newest and most dashing bathing suit, Tom had joined the others in the water and they were all tossing a ball about and ducking each other with much hilarity, none more energetically than he, which was rather curious, in view of his previous detachment. Moreover, he demonstrated himself to be a much superior swimmer to either of the boys, so it was clearly no place to convert Jane to the notion that she was wasting her time over a man twice her age and, after a token two lengths, I clambered out again and engaged in chatty conversation with Mrs Nicholson about her faded drawing room loose covers, forthcoming holiday in the Virgin Islands and the new man in London who was doing such marvels for her migraine.

All this was most agreeable and relaxing, but, as I was guiltily aware, hardly the purpose for which I had been invited.

Nor was there any question of staying for lunch, for the very simple reason that luncheon was not being served that afternoon. Mrs Nicholson quickly disposed of any such expectations by explaining that the boys were always so ravenous when they came out from school that she found it more practical to give them brunch the minute they entered the house. In this way, they had all the rest of the day to amuse themselves and work up an appetite for an early supper, before being transported back to their place of learning.

The single compensation here was that Tom, who had obviously also been counting on an invitation, eventually caught on and, back pedalling rapidly, muttered something about a luncheon engagement at the golf club with the old brigadier and of having, for his sins, promised to give him a round afterwards. It then dawned on him that he had no option but to offer me a lift home, about two seconds after it had dawned on me that I should have no hesitation in accepting.

"Which sins?" I asked him, as we hurtled down the Nicholsons' drive.

"Beg your pardon?"

"You said you had promised the brigadier 'for your sins'. I wondered what they were."

Absurdly enough, the distance by road to Toby's house was at least five times that of the footpath, although still not long enough for a moment to be wasted on meaningless civilities, specially with one who elected to drive at sixty miles an hour o'er hill and dale and hairpin bend.

"Oh, just a figure of speech, you know," he replied patronisingly. "Had you never heard the expression?"

"Yes, often; and, by the way, you may run across my husband at the golf club. He's the one called Price, you know. He's a Detective Inspector at Scotland Yard. I think it must be my long association with him which makes me take people so literally when they talk about their sins."

I could sense that he found this chatter distasteful and had also detected a flicker of apprehension ruffling his wooden features, so followed up the advantage by saying portentously:

"The fact is, you know, that people are apt to use

these clichés from a sub-conscious impulse. Guilt, I suppose it would be, in this case."

"Is that so? Well, my conscience is clear, thank you very much."

"Then you're lucky, but actually I was speaking of your sub-conscious conscience, not the one you carry around in the top of your head."

"What an extraordinary conversation, Miss Crichton, or are we Miss Price to-day? Do you make a habit of psycho-analysing virtual strangers with inquisitions on their private thoughts?"

"Not a habit, no."

"Then perhaps we could drop the subject? I find it intensely boring and I may as well add that I am not prepared to answer to you or anyone else for by sub-conscious."

"I don't see how you could be prepared for it. That would mean it wasn't really sub at all. However, what interested me was that when you made the remark we were sitting on the Nicholsons' terrace, slap in the middle of that fabulous view and it did occur to me that somewhere in the inner recesses of your mind there might be a twinge of guilt that you and Harry were proposing to ruin it."

I should have been more careful in my timing. Naturally, the object all along had been to needle him into a spontaneous response, but it might have been wiser to withhold the coup de grâce until we were safely round the approaching bend in the lane, or at least until he had slowed down to a suitable speed to negotiate it safely. I was in luck though, because to give him his due his loss of concentration was only fractional and although we came to rest with one wheel in the ditch, there was no danger to persons or property. Moreover, despite her querulous protestations, the fat woman on the bicycle who had been travelling towards us, having also ended in a ditch with the bike on top of her, was found to have sustained nothing worse than a nasty shock and a twisted handlebar.

"Sorry about that," Tom muttered, when he had got the car into a more respectable position on the grass verge and we had both lighted cigarettes to calm our flustered nerves. "Entirely my fault. Very sorry."

"Oh, that's all right."

"As a matter of fact, there was a bloody great stone in the road, about twenty yards back. Must have struck it, I think. Noticed it when you were calming down the old biddy. I must hand it to you there, by the way. Got her eating out of your hand in no time, by the look of it. Softened her up with a few digs about men drivers, I daresay?"

"No," I replied thoughtfully, "I don't think we referred to that at all. She just happened to have seen me on telly once or twice and it worked like a charm. Does come in handy sometimes when people recognise you."

"Must do," he replied through clenched teeth, re-starting the engine.

We covered the remaining mile and a half in silence and when I had thanked him for the lift and was getting out, the question which he had doubtless been phrasing and re-phrasing in his mind finally got its airing:

"By the way, did I dream it, or did you mention something back there about some building plans Harry has in mind?"

"No, you didn't dream it."

"Well, look here, no skin off my nose, I assure you, but I think it might be an idea to keep it under your hat

51

for the time being. Nothing to be gained by spreading it around the local gentry, if you see what I mean?"

"I do see what you mean, but Harry didn't asked me not to."

"May I know whether it would have made any difference if he had?"

"Yes, you may and yes, it would."

He was endeavouring to extricate another cigarette from his pack, but failing to make a clean job of it. His hand was shaking quite badly, possibly from delayed shock and I held out my own packet.

"No thanks, don't go for that brand. Well . . . um . . . sorry to harp on the subject, but I suppose you wouldn't be inclined to repeat exactly what Harry did tell you?"

"Why not ask him yourself?" I said, opening the door wide this time. "Goodbye and thanks again for the lift."

CHAPTER SIX

"Oldest trick in the world," I announced, sailing into Toby's study, where he was hard at work on *The Times* crossword. "You know what that is? Pretend to know something you don't and, quick as a flash, they tell you what it is."

"The telephone has been ringing," he replied gloomily, "four times since you went out. And, if I'm not mistaken, there it goes again."

"Where the hell have you been?" Anne squealed, "I've been trying to get you the whole morning. Six times at least and never any reply."

"Sorry, Anne, but something rather urgent came up and I had to go out. Toby doesn't always break off to answer the telephone when he's working. He would have, if he'd known it was you," I added hastily.

"But you promised faithfully to telephone me!"

"I know, and I would have this afternoon, but this really was quite important. All in the line of duty too, rest assured."

"How can it have been? And, anyway, I think it was jolly mean of you to walk out on us last night, particularly as you knew Harry was going to make a special announcement."

"Which I admit I was dying to hear, but you know as well as I do that he wouldn't have uttered a word in front of me. Cath was right there. The conversation would have been strictly confined to her saying: 'if you ask me' every two minutes, and Mary telling everyone she was awfully sorry, but . . ."

"I know. You can see why I find them so desperately tedious? Specially as nobody ever does ask Cath and, when you get right down to it, Mary's not sorry in the least."

"Besides," I added, realising that she had now worked off her ill humour, "I had my suspicions about what Harry was going to say and the confirmation has now come in, so nothing was lost."

"What's that? What are you on about now, Tessa? How could you possibly have guessed? I simply don't believe it!"

"Want to bet?"

"All right, prove it!"

"In one sentence: he intends to retrieve the family fortunes by turning Platts Meadow into a housing estate."

Such a long silence followed this announcement that I was afraid Anne had fainted, and it had apparently been a close thing because when she did speak again her voice sounded shaky and a little scared.

"How on earth, Tessa . . . ? Listen, are you a witch, or something?"

"So it is true?"

"Well, not exactly. I mean, not as terrible as you've made it sound, but you're on the right lines. What beats me is how you found out. None of the rest of us had a clue."

"I wouldn't depend on that," I told her, "I have a hunch there was one person who already knew quite a lot about it. And that's another reason why it would have been a waste of time my being there. Even if Harry had brought the subject up, I think the reaction from that quarter would have been quite carefully rehearsed."

"Well, you wouldn't have said so from the way they went on. Mary had screaming hysterics, for a start.

54

Admittedly, that happens every time the milk boils over, but this was different. She was genuinely upset, and you can understand it, in a way. It'll probably mean getting rid of the horses and trotting about on that old pony is practically her only pleasure in life. And Cath was worse still, in a way. Not so noisy about it, but white to the gills and she kept pacing up and down and saying that the only thing she had left which she valued at all was to be taken away from her and she'd be condemned to living in a nasty little country slum, with cars going past the cottage all day long and plastic flowers in the picture windows as far as the eye could see. You never heard such a performance. Harry kept trying to calm her down by explaining that it wouldn't be like that at all and, with all the lovely money he'd get, she could have her kitchen modernised, just like ours and Mary could have her own little car and perhaps go to some yummy old secretarial college in London; but it didn't do any good. You'd have thought they were both going to their executions. In the end I left them to it and went to bed."

"Very sensible! After all, it's only fantasy, isn't it? None of it could ever come true."

"On the contrary. I happen to know that Harry is dead serious and fully intends going ahead. And why the hell shouldn't he, if that's what he wants?"

"Because it's not a question of what he wants; he's living in a dream world. Doesn't he know that you have to get planning permission for these things? They're most frightfully tough about it too. You have to go on your knees in an area like this before they'll let you put up a rabbit hutch. Harry wouldn't get permission in a million years for a scheme like his."

This time there was an even longer silence at the other end and then Anne said slowly :

"So . . . there is something you don't know, after all!

He already has all the permission he needs. He's had it for over thirty years and he never even knew. His father got it for him."

"I don't believe it! He's bluffing!"

"No, it's all perfectly legal and above board. Tom's been in to it very carefully and you can bet your life he knows every trick in that trade. In fact, it was he who made the discovery in the first place. That was about three months ago and he and Harry have been working on it ever since."

"What discovery?"

"The one I'm telling you about. Apparently, when Harry's father built the cottage, the original plan was to put up three others nearby. It was a piece of cake in those days. All you had to do was prove that you needed houses for your farm labourers and bingo! Away you went."

"But in fact he only went away with one? I begin to see!"

"Right! Harry says the old man was terribly un-businesslike and probably hadn't a clue how much it was going to cost him; or maybe the war started and he hadn't any use for the others, but anyway he lost interest and the plans have been languishing in the files ever since. Naturally, everyone kept dead quiet about it and as the years went by they must have imagined they were safe; but they reckoned without our Tom. He was going through the archives one day, checking up on Common Rights or something, and he turned this up. After that, there was no stopping him."

"But surely, Anne, it can't still be valid after all this time? I thought these things lapsed automatically after a certain number of years?"

"In theory, they do, but Tom has friends in high

56

places, as you might have guessed, and he's pretty sure that he's got enough going for him here to push it through."

"And what about Harry? After all, it is his property and his responsibility."

"I know, but it's a bit complicated. He's absolutely broke, for one thing. The new kitchen worked out at about four times the original estimate. He hasn't even finished paying for the roof on that ghastly old pavilion yet and Cath never stops pleading for money. He says he'll never be able to afford the fees for Eton unless he can lay his hands on some capital and this would be one way of doing it. Listen, Tessa, I've been talking for hours and I've got to go now. I want to make sure Lizzie's all right."

"What have you done with her?"

"Left her in the pram under the big tree. She was asleep when I came indoors and Harry promised to keep an eye on her, but one can't trust him an inch. When can you come over? I know it's difficult for you when Robin's there, but how about Monday?"

"All right, if you say so, but do you really require my services any longer? I should have thought your own little personal problem would have been quite swallowed up in this giant, family sized drama?"

"No, it hasn't, and I'm feeling worse than ever. I'm absolutely stuck with the idea now that the two things are connected in some way. I need you more than ever, so come on Monday and don't dare let me down!"

"So there's one little mystery unveiled for you," I said, having reported back to Toby, "Harry has obviously realised that he's in for trouble with all you lot if he goes ahead with this rotten scheme, so he's trying to woo you with champagne and cream buns. That's the true reason why you've been fawned on."

"It will avail him nothing. Doesn't the poor fool understand what he'll be up against? It won't be brushed aside with a few hot dinners, I can tell you that much. He'll be ostracised and pelted with stones and black-balled from the Village Hall. We'll all be marching up and down his drive, bearing banners with rude slogans and singing 'We Shall Overcome' from dawn till dusk. Didn't you warn her about that?"

"Didn't get the chance. She had to break off in a hurry, to go and find out if anything terrible had happened to Lizzie."

"Was that likely? Where was Lizzie?"

"Asleep in her pram, under the big tree."

"Then what could have happened to her?"

"I couldn't tell you Toby, but you know what a maniac Anne is about that kind of thing? Perhaps she was afraid the tree had rotted while she was talking to me, and would fall down on the baby, cradle and all. Or perhaps she thought Lizzie might have been kidnapped. You know, some poor crazed woman who has lost her own child in the epidemic, wanders into the garden and is seized by the irresistible impulse."

"Yes, very possibly," Toby agreed, at precisely the moment when the telephone rang again.

I was beginning to have every sympathy with his complaints about the Purveyances. It might have been worth their while to have had a direct line installed.

They rang the changes too, as well as the numbers, and this time it was Harry. He sounded calm, but graver than usual and he wanted to know if Robin was available. I explained that we expected him back from the golf course at any minute and followed this up by asking if there was anything I could do in the meantime.

"No, I don't think so, my darling, thank you; not at this stage. Anne is in rather a frantic state, but Dr Bell is on his way, and if you'd just ask Robin to be very sweet and come over right away, the minute he gets back, I'd be eternally grateful."

Deeply alarmed, I could not resist badgering him for details and, by a very strange coincidence, he told me that they had reason to believe that Lizzie had been kidnapped.

CHAPTER SEVEN

Robin arrived home for the last time that evening at about ten, although we had been briefed with progress reports along the way and already knew by then that Lizzie had been found, safe and well and not much more than a thousand miles from home.

"Well done!" I said as he walked in. "If only all your cases could be dealt with so expeditiously, you'd be able to play golf every day."

"This one has hardly put me to the test," he replied, nevertheless pouring himself an extra stiff whisky. "The culprit's identity was never in much doubt, so it was a question of sorting out the various places where she might have taken the child and then going after her. Harry provided a list of possibles and we split them into three groups. Harry and I and that fellow, Tom, each took one, and Harry found her, which I think was also roughly according to plan. By that I mean that he'd dealt himself all the aces."

"What had made the culprit's identity so obvious?" Toby asked.

"Well, she'd left a note, you see; pinned to the baby's pillow, in the good old conventional style."

"In her own handwriting?"

"No, in capital letters and green ink. It stated that the child would be restored in one piece to her grateful parents as soon as Harry gave a written undertaking that he had relinquished all idea of building houses on Platt's Meadow, now or in the future. This to be handed in personally to the editor of the *Storhampton Gazette*.

The message purported to come from some rural conservation society, but Harry said he'd never heard of them and he was fairly confident he could recognise the little hand which had penned it. Naturally, though, at that point he wasn't banking on it."

"Although," I suggested, "if Mary had also absented herself, there couldn't have been much room for doubt?"

"Unfortunately, it wasn't as simple as that. She was known to have caught the ten thirty bus into Oxford and she wasn't expected back until late this evening. Her story was that she'd arranged to meet an old school friend and they were going to the early performance of some ballet company who are playing there this week. Cath said she even had her theatre ticket to prove it. She, of course, was very vehement about poor little Mary's innocence, right up to the end."

"And what was poor little Mary up to while she wasn't watching the ballet?" Toby asked.

"Playing with Lizzie in that macabre little building in the wood, which they call the pavilion. She'd set it up for a proper siege too; lots of toys, tinned food and blankets, even a change of clothes for the baby; she'd thought of everything. It was the ideal hiding place too because Harry's father used to camp out there on his bird watching nights and they've even got water laid on and a gas cylinder to cook by."

"Not only ideal," I said, "but singularly unenterprising as well. She'd made it so dead easy that I wonder Harry bothered to drag you in at all?"

"I think I was a sop, if you know what I mean?"

"No, of course I don't, Robin. That's the last word I'd use to describe you."

"Well, you can picture Anne's reaction when she discovered the pram was empty? No half measures there! She was not only positive she would never set eyes on her darling again, she was equally convinced that its poor mutilated body was already lying out on the Common and, in between bouts of screaming and tearing her hair over that, she was yelling at Harry to call the police immediately, so that they could set off in hot pursuit of the murdering kidnapper. Naturally, suspecting what he did, he was in no particular hurry to fall in with that idea; but on the other hand he had to find some way to pacify her until Dr Bell arrived with the sedatives. So I was brought in as a sort of token police force."

"And she's all right now, is she? No side effects?"

"Harry says she's so fuddled with all the pills that she's not making much sense at present; but no, it doesn't appear that any permanent damage has been done."

"She must be a lot tougher than she looks," I remarked. "Either that, or she's so determined to keep this baby that sheer will power sees her through every nerve-racking shock and strain."

"Which reminds me," Toby said. "How do you relate this latest prank to those other disasters? Is it one more episode in the campaign, or was Mary only concerned with throwing a spanner in her father's nasty works?"

"That's the question, isn't it? If someone has really been after Anne, this would seem to prove that it must have been Mary. On the other hand, Anne herself assured me that Mary was genuinely shocked and appalled when Harry dropped his bombshell last night, so perhaps there's no connection at all and it was pure coincidence that in trying to blackmail Harry, it was mainly Ann who suffered. Although," I went on, after a moment's thought, "it would not surprise me if Cath had already caught a whiff of what was in the wind. She's always been a great little eavesdropper and collector of gossip, in her sanctimonious way, and I'm pretty sure I caught her in the act yesterday evening. Now, where does that put us, I wonder?"

"You tell us," Toby said, "since you were going to, anyway."

"I'm not sure that I can, unless it suggests that Cath has been working from the opposite direction: in other words, striking at Harry through Anne. Because if she believed that Harry was also becoming obsessed by this idea of having a son and was trying to raise money chiefly on that account, then Cath might well have felt that her best bet was to remove any risk of that by ensuring that no child of either sex ever got born. How about that? Oh well, something to be working on, perhaps. One thing I do know for certain, though; whether this kidnapping was actually aimed at Anne or not, it won't do anything to improve her morale."

"And there's one thing I know for certain," Robin added, "which is that you're not going to spend the whole of to-morrow bolstering it up, whatever she says. In fact, you're not going near the place. To-morrow is my one whole day off in heaven knows how long and I've had my fill of the Purveyances for this weekend, at least."

"I love him when he does the masterful bit, don't you, Toby? To use your furniture analogy, it makes him look like a very stately Victorian tallboy. And you needn't worry, Robin, I never had any intention of going there to-morrow. We'll take the telephone off the hook, if necessary. I don't suppose my agent would be likely to ring me on Sunday."

CHAPTER EIGHT

No such drastic measures were needed, however, for it was another dry and sunny day and we spent most of it out of doors, lingering on in the garden until it was almost dark, and time for Robin to return to London.

When, by Monday morning, there had still been no word from the Purveyances, I began, such is the perversity of life, to be smitten by faint stirrings of guilt for having succeeded in putting them out of my mind for thirty-six hours and, to make amends, set out early to walk to Braithwaite House.

It was quiet and seemingly deserted when I arrived, with an almost eerie tidiness about it, which struck me as slightly sinister until I remembered that Monday was one of Mrs Chalmers' days and that she had doubtless been at work for a couple of hours already. Whereupon I promptly dropped the newspaper, which I had picked up for a glance at the headlines, replacing it, neatly folded, in its original position on the gleaming polished table. Just in time too, because a second later she entered by the back door, carrying an assortment of empty waste paper baskets and bins.

"Good morning, Madam," she said, returning my salutation. "Been out there making a good old bonfire with some of this rubbish."

"Oh, super!" I said fatuously.

The truth is that I stood in some awe of Mrs Chalmers who, despite her formal custom of addressing nearly everyone as Sir or Madam, was very conscious of her own importance and superiority. She had arrived on the scene before I was born, as housemaid in Harry's father's time, and had remained there ever since, in one capacity or another, a career which had not been noticeably interrupted by marriage or motherhood, and she rightly regarded herself as the prop and mainstay of the establishment. Now in her late sixties and well past retiring age, she was in fuller possession of herself and her faculties than ever, shrewd, outspoken, supercharged with energy and a demon for work. She was also, curiously enough, an enthusiastic primitive painter, a talent strongly encouraged by Harry, who provided her with all the materials for this hobby and had several examples of her work hanging in the house.

"Is Mrs Purveyance around anywhere?" I asked, having volunteered a few fulsome comments concerning the lovely shiny furniture and the advantages she must find in having such a splendid new kitchen to work in.

"Not here, Madam, not at this hour. She'd be over at the cottage, I'd have thought. Have you tried there?"

I was reminded that Mrs Chalmers strongly disapproved of Anne and the irregular relationship between her and Harry, although, strangely enough, his own part in this seemed to escape her censure altogether, and no doubt she regarded deed polls as less than the dust on the grand piano.

"I meant Mrs Anne Purveyance," I said humbly, nevertheless feeling an obligation to wave a tattered banner in defence of my friend.

"Oh, Miss Anne? She's still tucked up in her nice warm bed, if I know anything."

"Then I'll just buzz up and say hallo."

"Yes, you do that, Madam, and if you could get her moving I'd be much obliged. I'm about to have a go at the silver now, but after that's done I'll be ready to start on the bedrooms."

Mrs Chalmers had painted a very accurate picture this time, for Anne did indeed look extremely comfortable, propped up in the huge double bed and polishing off the remains of a delectable looking breakfast, Harry's work no doubt, on a tray across her legs. She also looked radiantly pretty and much more composed and serene than at our last meeting. In view of the fact that she had recently undergone a shock of such severity as would have shaken many a steelier nerve than hers, I found this a little odd; but she was not one to keep her own counsel for long and the explanation was soon forthcoming.

"You heard about our drama?" she asked, tossing a few magazines and newspapers on to the floor, to enable me to sit down on the bed.

"Yes, Robin gave us the whole story when he came home on Saturday night. It must have been horrible for you?"

"Yes, it was," she replied cheerfully. "The most horrible time I ever remember. I hope I never have to live through anything like that again, I can promise you."

"All the same, you seem to have come through it pretty well. You're looking very good."

"Am I?" she asked, smiling into her coffee cup. Then her expression changed, she put the cup down on the tray, leant back against the mountain of pillows and fixed me intently with her enormous dark eyes:

"To tell you the truth, Tessa, and I couldn't say this to anyone but you, but now that it's all over, I'm rather pleased it happened."

"Are you indeed? Well, there's a turn up for the book!"

"I know, and it's rather hard to explain, but I feel vindicated in a way. I've got something definite and tangible to complain about now, which I never had before."

"You astound me, Anne! I was under the impression that you had masses to complain about before."

"So I did, God knows I did, but there was nothing you could really pin down, if you can understand what I mean? I got absolutely sick to death of Mary romping about the house like some great overgrown puppy and yelling at the top of her lungs; and Cath was even worse, with her endless carping and criticism. I got so fed up with them that lots of times I felt like packing it in and running away."

"That I can understand."

"Yes, except that it was the very thing Cath was aiming and working for, which was one reason why I never did it. But the worst part was that Harry simply couldn't see it. They don't get on his nerves one bit, do you realise that? He's devoted to them, in his own peculiar way. Of course he feels guilty too, but it isn't only that. He's literally incapable of seeing their faults. Anyone who is related to him is okay and that's that. So when I complained, it was just draggy old me being mean and gripey."

"Even so, he doesn't lack imagination and it must have struck him occasionally how unnatural and tiresome it was for you to have his ex-wife and her daughter permanently warming their feet at your hearth?"

"Yes, it did and he admitted they could be interfering and tactless sometimes and didn't always understand that he and I might occasionally want to be on our own together, but he said there was another side to it too and that in lots of ways I'd be worse off without them."

"And how did he arrive at that comforting little theory?"

"He meant that I'd probably be bored to death, stuck

68

here in this deadly place, when he's working or riding and with no other woman to talk to, unless you count Mrs Chalmers ticking me off twice a week. He said that whether I liked it or not, I was the kind who needed female companionship and even the uncongenial variety was better than none."

"He may have a point there, Anne."

"Do you think so? Personally, I'd say he was rationalising, making it up as he went along; and the truth is I can't stand all this endless bickering. I'd swop it for loneliness any old day, but when I told him so, all he said was that instead of moaning about it I ought to cash in on the situation."

"And what did he mean by that?"

"That if I encouraged Mary a bit more she'd be perfectly willing to take Lizzie off my hands for a couple of hours every afternoon, so that I could put my feet up; and furthermore that she and Cath would jump at the chance to baby sit, so that he and I could go out on our own together in the evenings sometimes, which would kill two birds with one stone."

"And he certainly has a point there."

"He may have had at the time," Anne said with another of her radiant smiles. "Not that I see any reason why he should be pushed out of his own house, just so we can be alone, but the point is that even Harry wouldn't now expect me to hand Lizzie over to Mary for two minutes, after her performance on Saturday. Can you imagine? Goodness knows where they might both have got to by the time I took my feet down again!"

"Yes, I suppose that would be a slight complication."

"You bet it would, and I don't expect to be hearing any more about that charming idea in future. That's one good thing to come out of it and another is that it's given me a lovely new weapon against Cath."

"How's that?"

"Last night she had the abysmal cheek to start on one of her little lectures about child rearing and how I was spoiling Lizzie rotten by being over-protective and all the rest of it. You know the routine?"

"By heart."

"Exactly! So last night I got some of my own back. I said that anyone whose child had grown up to be capable of such a spiteful, vicious trick as Mary had just played was hardly in a position to hand out advice to other people. That shut her up. She went scarlet in the face and didn't utter another word. Even Harry looked slightly shaken. So you can see why I'm not truly sorry that Mary has gone and put her foot in it right up to her neck?"

"And do you expect to see less of them now, on that account?"

"Oh no, worse luck! At least, only for a few days. They'll soon gather round again, trying desperately to get back in favour, but the point is that they won't any longer have the upper hand."

"That still doesn't make you the winner, though. In all essentials, won't you be back where you started? Scarcely a meal that Cath and Mary aren't sharing with you? Or a moment, except when you're actually in bed, when you and Harry can be alone?"

Anne sounded positively triumphant in her response to this one :

"And that's where you make your biggest mistake of all, because you don't know half as much as you think you do. Oh, I'm sorry, Tessa," she went on in a gabble, looking contrite now and leaning forward to pat my hand. "Forgive me, for I shouldn't have said that, I know. You've been marvellously patient and sympathetic and I didn't mean to sound ungrateful. It's just that it's been such a rotten time all round and now everything's beginning to look so rosy, it's rather gone to my head."

"No need to apologise," I assured her, "I'm not offended in the least. Very few people know as much as they think they do and neither you nor I have ever been celebrated for it."

However, it appeared that nothing could ruffle her complacency that morning, for she grinned and patted my hand again, before gathering her white lace bed jacket around her and sinking back luxuriously against the pillows.

"Okay, okay, I said I was sorry. So stop being stuffy about it and listen to the rest of the news. You remember Jane Nicholson? She's Jane something else now, but you know who I mean?"

"Yes."

"And had you heard that she'd left that rat of a husband and come back to stay with her parents?"

"And got a job with your friend, Tom? Yes, I had."

"So you do know quite a lot, don't you, darling? Congratulations!"

"But that's about the sum of it; except that she and Tom are reputed to be slightly more than good colleagues. She's very beautiful, of course; there's that too."

"Oh, would you say so? Quite attractive, in her way, I suppose, but I hate that carroty colouring. It really turns me off people, as a rule. Still, that's only a personal opinion and the point is that Tom brought her here to lunch yesterday."

"Oh yes? And how did that go?"

"Like a great big beautiful bomb. Cath and Mary absented themselves for once, which is a good beginning for any party. Mary's too ashamed to show her face at the moment. It's rather comical really, because the latest idea she's got into that article she calls her head is that she's inherited her father's literary talent. She spends most of her time mooning about in the pavilion, writing her autobiography or something. Cath, on the other hand, is now taking the attitude that she refuses to set foot in the house when Tom's here, owing to his infamous and deceitful behaviour over the building plans. It won't last, unfortunately. They'll both climb down very smartly when they get really bored and hungry, but it did mean that for once we were able to have a proper conversation, instead of having to listen to all that self-centred tittle tattle. And Jane was simply marvellous with Lizzie; they took to each other on sight. Harry was in sparkling form too; really funny, like he used to be when I first met him. He'd cooked the most fabulous lunch and we sat over it until about four o'clock. He kept on opening more and more wine and in the end we were all slightly high. Tom was the worst and Harry said he could please himself about risking his own life, but he was in no state to drive Jane home and he insisted on taking her himself. Though, to tell you the truth, Tessa, I don't think he was in very good shape either. Still he got her there quite safely."

"Sunday orgies in the Green Belt! And what was the upshot of all this? Or don't you remember?"

"I remember perfectly; not the faintest trace of a hangover, I'd like you to know. As a matter of fact, I didn't drink nearly as much as the others because I had to leave them for about an hour, while I was putting Lizzie down to rest; and that's when they fixed up this marvellous plan."

"What marvellous plan?"

"About Jane coming to give us a hand sometimes. Apparently, while I was upstairs she said something about what a jolly shame it was that I had to leave the party and how would it be if she came round in the afternoons sometimes for an hour or two, to take Lizzie for a walk, or play with her in the garden, so that I could have some time off?"

"I thought she was supposed to be working for Tom?"

"So she is, but you know as well as I do that it was mainly an excuse to get out of her parents' clutches. I don't imagine she sees it as a great career and Tom said it would be quite okay for her to go on to a part time basis, if she wanted to. Mornings only, or whatever."

"Do you think he's in love with her?" I asked, recalling his impassive behaviour at the swimming pool.

"You know, I wondered about that myself, Tessa, but in the end I decided he wasn't, not one bit. I was watching them during lunch. I know Tom is rather a graven image, but he hardly looked at her and he never made any protest when Harry insisted on driving her home."

"In that case, don't you find it rather puzzling that he allows himself to be used in this way? Giving her a job for which she is totally unfitted, in the first place, and then calmly saying that she can more or less come and go as she pleases?"

"No, not particularly. He's a crashing snob and he probably sees her as adding a bit of class to the business. I bet you anything he makes a point of taking her along when he's got some really big fish coming to view a place, so that she can chat them up about how convenient it is for Ascot and all that. In any case, what do I care why he does it? All that matters is that she's someone I can get on with and would trust implicitly with Lizzie. What's more, she says that if it all goes smoothly she'd be willing to come and baby-sit in the evenings once in a while and that's what I really call killing two birds with one stone. And now the hellish thing is that I suppose I'd better drag myself out of bed and have a bath. Otherwise, Mrs Chalmers will be bullying me about getting in here to do the room. Be an angel, Tessa, and cast an eye on Lizzie when you go down, will you? She's in the garden with Harry. I don't think he'd dare leave her for a second, after our recent experience, but one can't ever absolutely depend on anything where he is concerned."

It would be wrong to describe my friend, Anne, as a manic depressive, or at any rate only as one of the most lopsided variety, for the ratio was approximately one to ninety-nine per cent. Such flashes of pure, unadulterated happiness as I had just witnessed were not only rare, but apt to be of extremely short duration. I was all too well aware that it only needed a sharp word from Mrs Chalmers, or the discovery that the bath water was cold, for this one to drown in a sea of pessimism and was careful not to hasten the process by making any reference on this occasion to the real or imaginary attempts on her life. I refrained from pointing out that if either Cath or Mary had been responsible for these, as she herself patently believed, then there was no great cause for celebration. Temporarily driven back into their corners as they might be by Mary's ridiculous blunder, it was still almost inevitable that the guilty one would strike again as soon as an opportunity presented itself.

CHAPTER NINE

There was no sign of either Harry or Lizzie when I walked into the garden from the drawing room, so I continued on round to the far side of the house, where the library, which was also the room where Harry worked, and sacred to that small and intermittent activity, overlooked a broad grass walk between the two herbaceous borders. The sun had not yet reached it and in the heavy dew which still lay thickly on the grass were impressions of two thin parallel lines which could only have been made by the wheels of a pram.

I followed them down to the end of the walk, which, as I knew, eventually narrowed into a footpath through the copse, and here the trail ended. There was only one inference to be drawn, since what went up had certainly not come down, so I went on along the path for another quarter of a mile or so, to the point where it joined up with a cart track, separating the wood from Cath's garden, digressing at the half-way point for a brief inspection of the pavilion, so-called, which had been Mary's H.Q. in the abduction campaign.

It stood in a small clearing, a circular wooden building, about eight feet in diameter, with a tiny iron spiral staircase going up through the centre of it and a pointed roof, newly thatched now and looking exactly like a giant, inverted ice cream cone. It had been built to the exact specifications of Harry's father, who was not only eccentric and unbusinesslike, but also a dedicated bird watcher, and had frequently spent whole nights there when conditions were propitious. This was the reason, I had been told, for its having been constructed on two levels, the lower one fitted out as a rough, camper's kitchen and the upper being just large enough for a chair, a table for recording notes on and a camp bed. It may have accounted for the fact that the entrance was in the form of a stable door, with bolts and padlocks outside, providing ventilation when the top half was open, the only windows being tucked high up under the eaves.

From the other side of Cath's hedge, when I reached it about ten minutes later, came the whining strains of a mowing machine, evidently on its last legs and when I went through the gate and into the garden I saw that the operator was Mary, whose legs also looked as though they might give way at any moment. She was pounding up and down, scarlet in the face and having to break off every two or three minutes to regain her breath and push the hair away from her streaming eyes.

It was, in fact, only a tiny lawn, not more than three times the size of an average room, but the need for the appalling effort came from the fact that the ground sloped down from the house in a gradient of about one in five, and the grass had been allowed to grow too high and to become choked with sturdy looking plantains. It was also soaking wet and it struck me that only Mary would elect to undertake such a task in those conditions.

Perhaps she had done so to impress her father, for Harry was also walking up and down, although in a more relaxed and leisurely fashion. A horizontal strip of meadow, adjoining the garden, had been fenced off to make a paddock, the domain of a mournful and prim looking goat named Elsa and kept there for the benefit of Cath who, for some reason concealed from me to this day, was unable to drink cow's milk. Harry was strolling back and forth along this paddock, with one arm wrapped around Lizzie, who was perched on the donkey's back.

The only sedentary member of the party was Cath, reclining in a deck chair and clicking away at her pink knitting, who graciously offered me a sugar biscuit from a plate beside her outstretched legs.

"Strictly speaking, they're specially for Lizzie," she explained. "A secret little tin I keep hidden away for when Harry brings her to visit me."

All this was said in a simpering, wistful tone, as though to imply that she could not afford such luxuries for herself and Mary, but I suspected that the secret tin might also be a secret weapon in the battle to undermine Anne, who doubtless held the most stringent views about sugary snacks between meals.

I thanked her and accepted the offer, at the same time sinking into the second deck chair. Whereupon Mary, evidently maddened by the sight of yet another individual taking it easy, jerked her machine sideways and came and flopped down on the grass at our feet, panting loudly and saying she was awfully sorry, but she couldn't carry on a minute longer, not unless we all wanted her to drop dead, though without waiting to hear whether we did or not.

I noticed that she cast predatory glances at the biscuits, but she was not offered one, so it must have been unbearably frustrating for her when, a few minutes later, Harry having set the donkey free and brought Lizzie over to join us, she not merely refused to be tempted, but recoiled in disgust at the sight of them. It ended with Harry scoffing the lot, saying what blissful bickies they were, putting Cath through an inquisition on what they were called and where she had bought them and reminding himself several times over to tell Anne to include them in her next grocery order.

"And I am reminded of something too," I told him, "Anne will be out of her bath by now and is probably looking for you. I have been delegated to keep you under observation."

"Yes, quite right! Time to go home now Liz-biz. And you must come with us, Tessa heart, and stay to lunch."

"No, thanks. I'll walk as far as your house and then I'm going home."

"Oh, you can't, you can't! We're having *moules marinières*, all hygienically scrubbed by Mrs Chalmers. Besides, Anne doesn't see nearly enough of you, now that you're rich and famous. She's devoted to you, you know."

"No, she's not. We've known each other for a very long time and she's used to me, that's all."

"Well, it's the same thing, isn't it, my darling?" he said, picking Lizzie up and tossing her into the pram, "Come along, now! Goodbye, girls! And don't give yourself a heart attack over that grass, my darling Mary. You'd better come over some time and borrow that rotary thing."

"Oh, thank you, Daddy, that would be marvellous. You are a poppet! The only thing is, though . . ."

"What?"

"I'm awfully sorry, but it's so heavy, I don't see how I'll be able to lug it here on my own."

"Oh, never mind that. We'll arrange it somehow. Off we go now, you two! Best foot forward!"

The path through the wood was not wide enough for two people to walk abreast, so Harry went ahead with the pram, talking and singing to Lizzie as he bumped it over the rough track, and when he reached the grass walk and I caught up with them again I saw that her head had lolled sideways and that she had fallen asleep.

"It's the riding that does it. Completely whacked, poor girl," Harry explained, straightening her out in a competent and practised fashion. "Never mind, we'll wheel the pram under the big tree, where you and I will sit beside it, talking very quietly, and then Mummie can look at us from her bedroom window and see how good we're all being."

"Just as well, really," he added, when we had taken up these positions. "One can never be quite sure how much a child of two can make of an adult conversation. It would sometimes seem that if they can grasp so easily that a train is called a puffer, when trains haven't puffed for two generations, nothing at all is beyond their comprehension, and one wouldn't want to take any chances."

"Why is that?" I asked. "Are we to be confidential as well as quiet?"

"Yes, exactly! I have a question for your ears alone."

I waited for it in silence and after a while he went on :

"As we were just saying, you and Anne have been friends for a very long time. You probably understand her better than any of us. Do you think she would go for money, rather than respectability, or vice versa?"

"I don't think she has ever been faced with the choice," I answered in some astonishment. "Why is it important for you to know?"

"Because she is about to be faced with it now and it would be helpful to gauge her reactions in advance."

"Am I to understand that the question has some connection with those rotten little houses with which you propose to disfigure Platt's Meadow, given half a chance?"

"Ah, so she's told you about them, has she?" he asked, evidently not at all offended by these frank words.

"Well, I'm glad of that because it saves no end of bother. And you're quite right, my dearest, it has everything to do with them. I find myself in rather deep water, I must tell you."

"And the tide will not be going out just yet."

"No, it won't, Cassandra dear. While my little patch of dry sand oozes away. Ultimatums on all sides."

"Ultimatums, Harry?"

"On all sides. From Tom, who has invested the best months of his life and thousands from his own pocket, I am given to understand, only to be faced with the prospect of all the profits going down the drain. If I drop the scheme now he will probably sue me for loss of business, breach of promise and a nervous breakdown. As though I cared! And, besides, he would never dare. But Cath now! Cath is a much more daunting kettle of fish."

"And what is Cath's ultimatum?"

"In direct conflict with the other, as you have already guessed. If I refuse to abandon the scheme she will remove herself and Mary to another part of the country, far beyond my reach. Her cottage must be sold, she says, and the money used to procure her another, in some situation where the vandals have not been at work. All she asks from life now is beauty and peace, and if they are not available here she must seek them elsewhere."

"And you wouldn't care for that?"

"I shouldn't care for it at all; and I don't think it would be entirely fair to Mary, who has not had the best of deals and may not be quite ready yet to sacrifice everything for the sake of peace and beauty."

"Does the cottage belong to Cath?"

"Only for her lifetime. Technically speaking, it is still my property, but I can't see what difference that makes.

80

You are not suggesting that I could allow them to be homeless, even in another part of the country?"

"No, I suppose not, but I must be fairly dim because it sounds to me as though Anne's choice lies between lots of money and no Cath, or lots of Cath and no money. I can't see where respectability comes into it."

"That is because you haven't heard my own ultimatum."

"You have one too?"

"The pick of the bunch, in a way. After delivering hers, Cath had the grace to admit that she would only put it into action with the greatest possible reluctance and she asked me if there were any single persuasion, compromise, bribe or quid pro quo I cared to name, which would induce me to call it off and allow us all to go on living as we do now, and I replied that there was."

"You did?"

"I did. With Anne, and to some extent our unborn son in mind, I told Cath that if she would consent to a divorce and enable me and Anne to be married, I would forget the whole business and never again refer to it by word or deed."

"And what did she say to that?"

"She hasn't given me her final answer yet. She said she would require notice of the question, but I have little doubt what the outcome will be. She has strong religious views, so she tells me, but I should be surprised if the need for peace, beauty and her present style of life did not exert an even stronger pull. So now all we need to know is how Anne will feel about it. Being married to me may not be the most enviable position for a woman, but it might be better than her present one. You agree?"

"Oh, I suppose it would. Yes, undoubtedly."

"And you consider that Anne will view it in the same

light? That she would accept my hand, and to hell with the money?"

"How can you ask such questions when you must know that it will depend entirely on yourself?"

"Not at all, not at all, my darling. I thought I had stated my position clearly. Whichever way it goes, I am bound to lose something; either what I possess already, or what I was hoping to gain. It will be for Anne to choose."

"Oh Harry, what an ass you are sometimes! Hasn't it sunk in yet that Anne is demented about you, would go to the stake for you?"

He waited, not answering, so I crossed the T's:

"Why else would she have put up with your eccentric, selfish and slightly unwholesome design for living for all these years?"

"Not without a certain amount of grumbling, I must tell you."

"Maybe not, but grumbling was where it began and ended. No foot stamping ultimatums there, you notice? And the answer to your question is that she will do precisely what she has always done, which is whatever you want. In other words, you will make the bed and she will lie on it. I, personally, don't believe she cares such a hell of a lot about money, but if she's convinced that you do, then believe me, old boy, you're going to be rich."

Having shot this bolt, I did not consider that I could improve matters by pushing it home any further and I went back to Toby's house to open a book with him.

He disagreed emphatically with my main premise, insisting that it was much more likely that Anne would follow whichever line suited her herself and then con Harry into the belief that this had been his own choice all along. However, it must be admitted that he does not always rate female integrity very highly.

"Okay," I said. "So what's the betting?"

"Since you tell me that the choice lies between marriage without money and money without Cath, I will give you twenty to one that she goes for the second. She would be a fool not to."

"You're on!" I told him, "and I'll hold you to it, if I win because I deserve to, mine being the more charitable view. It is my bet that she will settle for penury and marriage, partly because she yearns for those legal chains, but mainly because in her heart she knows that the one thing really to destroy Harry would be the break up of his beloved family."

"Then she most certainly is a fool," he replied. "Specially in view of her strong hints that one member of his beloved family has been trying to kill her. Incidentally, Tessa, how is that vendetta getting along? I don't seem to have heard much about it lately."

"I suppose it has been overshadowed; which may indicate that it never existed at all and that Anne's febrile mind has to have something to chew on, and when nothing dramatic is occurring her imagination leaps in to fill the void. On the other hand," I went on, giving him a grave and ominous look, "if it was true and if Mary's kidnapping stunt was one more move in the game, then. . . ."

"Then it would be as well to lose your bet?"

"Precisely! Whatever Mary's incentive may have been for trying to wipe out Anne, or the new baby, or both, it is unlikely to go away when news reaches her that her parents are to be divorced and she and her mother to be supplanted by Anne and Lizzie."

CHAPTER TEN

In a sense, we both won and both lost, for when the time came for a settlement the outcome was one which, however often we had skirted around it, neither of us had actually predicted, and if we had had the heart to refer to our wager again we should have been obliged to declare both horses non-runners.

Not that this was apparent in the early stages, for about three weeks after my talk with Harry, when I was back in London rehearsing for a new production, I had a telephone call from Anne which, whatever misgivings it may have aroused on her behalf, certainly enhanced my own hopes of winning twenty pounds. She told me, in strictest confidence and on pain of death not to breathe a word to anyone, that Cath had consented to a divorce and that it was to be pushed through with the utmost speed, to enable the baby to be born in wedlock.

"Congratulations!" I said, "I know it's what you've always wanted and I'm delighted for you, but why all the secrecy?"

"Well, mainly because a lot of people round here don't realise we aren't married already and, with the exception of Mrs Chalmers, those who did have more or less forgotten; so we don't particularly want to rake it up again. Also there's Mary."

"Oh yes, Mary! What about her?"

"She hasn't been told yet. She's bound to be distraught and Harry wants to break it to her in his own time."

"Well, my goodness, Anne, that's a bit optimistic,

isn't it? Mary may be slightly retarded, but not as infantile as all that, surely? She's bound to find out, and probably has already."

"I doubt that. She only got back last night."

"Back? Where from?"

"She's been away for ten days, didn't you know? Well, no reason why you should, really, I suppose."

"Where did she go?"

"To stay with some woman Jane knows, who breeds poodles. I forget her name, but she lives near Chelmsford. Anyway, the kennel maid, or whatever they're called, broke her arm and Jane had this brilliant idea for Mary to go and help out during the crisis."

"It sounds as though Jane is rapidly becoming indispensable on all fronts?"

"You're so right, Tessa, and it's rather getting on my nerves. It's not that I don't like her, because I honestly do and so does Harry. She's absolutely divine with Lizzie and she's always coming up with these bright ideas. One can't exactly fault her."

"So what's unnerving about it?"

"Just that she's inclined to take a damn sight too much on herself sometimes . . . and . . . well, to be frank, Tessa, I hadn't expected to see quite so much of her. I thought it would be just for a couple of hours in the afternoon and perhaps an occasional evening, but she seems to spend most of her time here nowadays and of course her parents encourage it like mad. They consider it to be so much more suitable to be here with us than working for Tom. But she can be awfully bossy at times and it's really getting to be a bore."

"It sounds as though, instead of solving your problems, she's busy creating a few fresh ones."

"Oh well, perhaps it will sort itself out when we're actually married and I can organise things more my own way. And that reminds me, Tessa: I haven't really rung you up to complain about Jane, I want you and Robin to be witnesses at our marriage."

"When is it?"

"We can't fix the exact date yet. It depends on the decree coming through, but roughly the second or third week of October."

"So long as it isn't a matinée day I'll be happy to oblige. That is, if we haven't folded by then," I added, wishing that telephone receivers were made of wood, so that I didn't need to put the receiver down, in order to clutch the table with both hands. "You'd better not count on Robin, though. The criminal classes are apt to be unpredictable in their timing and he might be forced to let you down at the last minute."

"Well, be a love and ask him anyway, will you? I'd rather have Robin, but I suppose if he does find he can't make it, your cousin wouldn't mind stepping into the breach?"

"Toby? I could ask him to stand by, I suppose . . . except . . . are you having a party afterwards?"

"My God, Tess, you must be joking! Apart from everything else, I'll be about seven months gone by then. We'll probably have a drink in some pub afterwards and then go straight home."

All this was recited rather in the style of the *One Note Samba*, for although the lyric was inoffensive the tune was decidedly cheerless. Even the topic of her approaching marriage had done nothing to lighten it and so after a slight hesitation I said:

"You don't sound particularly enchanted by the prospect. Isn't it what you've always hoped for?"

"Oh sure! Yes, of course it is and I'm chuffed as anything, but somehow or other, when you've looked forward to something for ages, it hardly ever turns out to be such a riot when you get it. For one thing, it usually means giving up something else. Not that I feel at all confident yet that I actually will get it, I may as well tell you."

"Why not? You aren't suggesting that Harry would back out at this stage?"

"No, nothing like that. I just feel that . . . well, that there are forces working against me, if you like."

"Oh Anne, honestly!"

"It's easy for you to laugh, you're not stuck here in the thick of it. I've got a sixth sense about these things and I feel as though I were surrounded by enemies on all sides."

On reflection, I was obliged to concede that no sixth sense was needed to recognise the truth of this, for it was not to be expected that Cath would feel any more fondly towards her for having usurped her own position, or that Mary would be over-burdened with gratitude either, when the time came for her to learn about it. Nor did it need much imagination to foresee that Tom would also be blaming her for the frustration of his financial hopes; but my job was to accentuate the positive and I said:

"Never mind, Anne, there's not so long to go now. Waiting is always the hardest part and you're bound to feel better when this tiresome interim period is over."

I could picture the tears of self-pity welling up in her eyes, for they spilled over into her voice as she answered tremulously:

"No, it isn't. The hardest part of all is never knowing when I wake up in the morning whether I'll still be alive at the end of the day."

I put a hand over the receiver, in order to indulge myself in a long drawn out groan, before replacing it once more on the plough:

"Am I to understand there have been some more of those disagreeable incidents?"

"Yes, you are. At least, I think so. One, at any rate."

"What happened this time?"

"I'd rather not tell you over the phone. It frightens me to talk about it when I'm alone here. You couldn't come down, I suppose? I mean, I know you're working now, but how about the weekend? You don't rehearse on Sundays, do you?"

"Not often, but . . ."

"Then couldn't you come down? Please, Tessa, do say you will! It would make the whole difference, and you did tell me once that you had a standing invitation to stay with Toby whenever you liked, so I'm sure you could fix it, if you tried. It would be such a comfort to have you here, even for twenty-four hours."

"All right, Anne, I'll do my best, but not next week-end. Robin has some time off, for once in his crowded life and we mean to jaunt about together, all on our own. I might manage the following one."

"Oh, marvellous, Tessa, will you really? Oh, you are a love! I can't tell you what a relief it is to hear that."

I noticed that she did not appear to have any qualms about her ability to stay alive for another ten days, but it is always flattering to find oneself so much in demand, however inappropriately, and I promised to get in touch with Toby, while she continued to pour out her gratitude.

Just before ringing off, I said:

"If it's any consolation to you, we do seem to be inching forward slightly in the process of elimination."

"How do you make that out?"

"Well, at least we can be certain now that it's not Harry who is secretly trying to break your neck with plastic balls. I mean, he would scarcely go to all the bother and expense of getting a divorce unless he visualised your being alive to benefit by it, would he?"

"Of course it's not Harry. I always told you that and I do wish you'd get that stupid idea out of your head, once and for all."

"Okay, okay, only my joke. What's more to the point is that we also now know that it can't be Mary either."

"Why can't it?" she asked sharply.

"I thought you told me she'd been away for ten days and didn't get back until last night?"

There was silence and when Anne's voice came back on the line it held the faintly triumphant note which I had noticed in it several times before when she was scoring points, particularly those which counted against her.

"Yes, that's right, but the fact is, Tessa, it doesn't necessarily prove a damn thing. It could still have been Mary who was responsible last time, and all the other times as well. You'll understand why when I tell you about it."

CHAPTER ELEVEN

Exactly one week later, during a lunch-break prowl through the gift department of a London store, I was struck for the fiftieth time by the fact that the shops are always crammed with gorgeous and appropriate wedding presents until the day arrives when you actually know someone who is getting married. A friend of mine, incidentally, who has two daughters aged six and four, informs me that a similar rule applies when she has to buy clothes for them. The only attractive garments on sale are all for children aged two and eight.

I had moved in desperation to the kitchenware section and was examining a set of Scandinavian enamelled saucepans of the colour and price of rubies, when another roseate object caught my eye, which was the back of Jane Nicholson's head. She held a soufflé dish in each hand, one plain white and the other decorated with radishes, and was gazing from one to the other in a pensive manner.

"Surely people don't any longer make soufflés, do they?" I asked her, "I thought it all depended on a well trained liaison officer telling them that dinner is served, Madam, and making damn sure they jumped to it?"

"They're quite useful for trifles and things like that," she replied, not bothering to name anything which was quite like a trifle, "are you on this kick too? What a bore, isn't it? I'm inclined to give up the whole idea and get my mama to find something suitable. She's quite bright at that sort of thing. Let's go upstairs and have some coffee?"

"All right, if you can wait five minutes. I'm spending next weekend there and these saucepans will be going with me. At least, I'll save myself a few hundred pounds in postage."

I noticed that she gave me a startled look and, when we had tracked down an assistant who, having nothing more amusing to do at the time, graciously consented to wander off in search of a pen and order book, Jane said:

"Spending next weekend where?"

"Roakes, of course; with Toby. These are for Harry and Anne's new kitchen. You know, wedding present."

In saying this I had not forgotten that I had been sworn to secrecy on the subject, but had concluded from various of Anne's remarks concerning Jane, including most particularly the ruse to get Mary bundled off to Essex, that the ban did not extend to her.

"Isn't that who you were buying your trifle dish for?"

"Good God, no. Mine was a present for a cousin who lives in Scotland; and, if I were you, Tessa, I'd stick those saucepans right back where you found them. Go on, quick, before she catches you!"

I hadn't been all that demented about them, anyway, and there was an urgency in Jane's voice which could not be denied. I replaced the saucepans on the shelf, alongside their royal blue brothers and sisters, and we scampered towards the lifts.

"You mean, you haven't heard about all the rumpus?" she asked, as we travelled up to the fifth floor.

"No. What rumpus?"

"Tell you later," she replied, directing a barrage of meaning glances at our fellow passengers, who appeared to be totally unaware of our existence and probably didn't speak English, in any case.

"What rumpus?" I asked again, when she had made her choice between three empty tables and ordered the coffee. I was turning mutinous by this time and in full sympathy with Anne's complaints about her bossiness.

"Funny," she remarked, idly studying the menu card, "I'd have expected you to be among the first to hear, you being such an old friend and everything."

"Well, Robin and I were out practically every minute last weekend, and we both have to leave the house very early on working days, so they may have tried to telephone, for all I know, but do get on with it, Jane, and tell me what's happened."

"Anne's had a miscarriage, that's what."

"Oh no! My God, how terrible! Poor Anne! Is it true?"

"You bet. I was there while it was all going on; or most of it, at any rate. They carted her off to Storhampton Memorial Hospital. Don't look so doomed! It was quite a bad haemorrhage, but she's recovering. They'll probably let her out in a few days."

"Well, that's something. But why aren't you there, helping out?"

"Because Cath gave my my congé, that's why. She came up with some pretty little story about how it would be best for Lizzie not to have too many people chivvying her around while she goes through this traumatic experience of being deprived of her mother, and that I should fade out for a bit. Cath's in her element, as you can imagine?"

"So well! And it's all too wretched and beastly for words. When did it happen?"

"Few days ago. Last Saturday morning was when it started."

"Well, go on! How did it start?"

"In the most ridiculous way imaginable," Jane replied, looking faintly amused by the absurdity of it, "it was that old goat who caused all the trouble. Anne had taken

93

Lizzie down to see the horses, but Mary was exercising the pony, so there was only one of them on view. She was standing in the paddock, holding Lizzie up and both of them feeding it with lumps of sugar, and the goat came up and butted her in the behind."

"That silly old Elsa? But she's usually such a docile creature!"

"Perhaps Cath had laced her drinking water with gin or something, but anyway it was quite a biff and Anne started yelling blue murder. Lizzie likewise, because in all the confusion she'd fallen on the other side of the fence and they were both terrified out of their wits. Eventually, Cath heard them and came to the rescue."

"Why eventually? If they were making all that din, why didn't she come at once?"

"It seems she was listening to a music programme on the radio and she'd got it turned up rather loud, while she went pattering round the house with her duster. She says she did hear a bit of screaming at one point, but she'd already seen them in the paddock and she took it they were just laughing in a rather hysterical fashion. Anyway, it finally dawned on her that there was something a bit unnatural about it, so she went out to investigate. Anne was on her feet by that time, trying to clamber over the fence to get to Lizzie. She says it must have been at least ten minutes before Cath arrived on the scene, but Cath says: 'Oh no, it couldn't have been half as much; nearer three, if you ask me.' "

"So then what?"

"She took them up to the cottage. Anne insisted on carrying Lizzie, which was probably a bad thing to do in the circumstances, and Cath gave her a slug of brandy to pull her together, which was also not terribly bright, according to my Ladies' Manual on Abortions. Then they thought she ought to lie down, but the poor little rickety

94

sofa in Cath's mean little sitting room was far too uncomfortable, so they were both escorted upstairs to her bedroom and there they stayed until Harry arrived to fetch them home."

"And how long did that take?"

"Quite a while, actually," Jane admitted. "Unfortunately, no one had the remotest idea where he'd got to. I was on my own there when Cath telephoned to report. Tom had dropped me off at the house and then gone out to look for Harry, having matters to confer with him about. When she told me that things were a bit strained, I went out to see if I could find them, but no luck. However, it seems that Mary got home from her ride soon after that, and she'd seen Harry, all on his own, near the pavilion, so she went chasing after him. He carried Anne home and put her to bed and an hour or two later the fun started."

"Was the baby formed enough for them to be able to tell its sex?"

"At five months? You bet it was!"

"And?"

"A boy. Wouldn't you know? So now you've heard all the gory details. Want some more coffee?"

"Not quite all," I told her, pushing my cup forward, "but enough to be getting on with, I suppose."

"Why? What have I left out?"

"I'm not sure, Jane. I just have this odd feeling that there's something missing somewhere. It's a pity that no one else actually saw that episode with the goat."

"Why? What on earth difference would that have made?"

"None, I suppose; you're right. And I'm really grateful to you for not letting me buy those saucepans. There'd have been something horribly inappropriate about them, in the circumstances. Still, it has only shelved the problem, hasn't it? Presumably, there won't any longer be this mad rush to get married, but once she's on her feet again I suppose plans will go ahead? I'll still be stuck with finding a wedding present."

"I wouldn't be in too much of a rush over that, if I were you," Jane said, looking down her finely chiselled nose.

"Oh? Why not?"

"I have a feeling Harry may not be so keen about getting himself tied down, now that this has happened."

"Oh, really? That wasn't the impression I got. He gave me to understand he was doing it principally for Anne's sake. I don't see why losing the baby should make any difference."

"That's because you haven't heard the sequel."

I sighed: "Oh, there's a sequel, is there? I was rather afraid of that."

"Why?" she asked sharply, "you mean you've heard about that squalid little scandal?"

"No, what scandal?"

"Then why were you afraid there'd be a sequel?"

"I honestly can't tell you, Jane, but perhaps that's what I meant by there being something missing. The story seemed unfinished in some way. Maybe because nothing in that household ever seems to occur as an isolated event. There are always repercussions."

"There've been repercussions this time, all right, and they're still thundering on."

"Something to do with the baby being a boy?"

"You could say that. Naturally, it made it all the more fraught. They were both dead keen to have a son and they were both counting on it, for some reason."

"I know."

"And they were right, you see, Tessa, which probably goes to show that one shouldn't scoff at these premonitions. Not that it affects me, one way or the other, since I don't ever intend to have any children. And that reminds me. I must go in five minutes, if not sooner. I've got an appointment with my lawyer. Charles and I are definitely packing it in, you know."

"Tell me about the repercussions," I said, unwilling for her to waste a single one of the five on her own boring marital troubles.

"Yes, well, you see, everyone was prepared for Anne to go round the bend when she heard it was a boy she'd lost, but they hadn't expected Harry to be almost as bad. He was absolutely distraught, poor old Harry, couldn't snap out of it at all. Tom said he'd never seen him so got down by anything, but Cath told me she had, just once before, when his mother died."

"Ah, Cath! I thought she'd come into it sooner or later."

"Well, when you get right down to it, she has known him longer than any of us and she told me that although his mother had always been fairly foul to him, he went all to pieces when she died. It was quite a serious breakdown and that was why Cath was worried this time. She recognised the signs."

"Oh yes?"

"You sound sceptical, darling! Why should that be, I wonder?"

"Stop wondering and get on with the story!"

"Well, as it happens, I'm with you in finding Cath a creaking old bore most of the time, and also she can be extremely bitchy in her quiet way, but you'd grant that she had some excuse if you'd heard her side of the story. Anyway, the point is that, in spite of everything, she's still devoted to Harry and I'm sure she was being sincere when she said how anxious she was for him. Which is why she'd made up her mind, however much it went against the grain, to pass on some information she'd got from Tom."

"That's funny," I said, digressing in spite of myself, "she was once on the brink of passing on some information to me which she'd got from Tom. I bet she would have too, if I'd pressed her. I wonder if it was the same bit?"

"Unlikely, because this was a real, flaming old hot potato and she swore that nothing would have induced her to unseal her lips if she hadn't truly believed that it would help to jerk Harry out of his miseries. The truth being that there was an even chance that the child wasn't his at all. I mean, that he wasn't the father."

"And now I'll grant you that I have heard everything," I said, starting to laugh. "Good old Cath! She never gives up."

"It's not quite so funny as you appear to think," Jane said, looking piqued by my merriment.

"You're right; it's not in the least funny, it's sheer, raving lunacy, and also preposterous and rather wicked. If there's one self-evident truth in this world it is that Anne and Harry are potty about each other and that she hasn't looked at another man since she first clapped eyes on him."

"That happens to be your opinion, and no doubt it's what she's told you, but it isn't borne out by the facts."

"Facts, I presume, being your way of describing some stupid, malicious invention of Tom's, who's always trying to mix it because he loathes Anne and recognises her as the main obstacle in his campaign to manipulate Harry for his own ends. I apologise for being offensive about your dear friend and current employer, but the fact is that he's a greedy, mischief making, spurious upstart."

"Oh, go ahead and enjoy yourself! I don't hold any particular brief for him. He's been fantastically kind to me, for reasons which may not be particularly praise-worthy and, having seen him in operation, I wouldn't trust him an inch in any business deal. All the same, I don't believe he's capable of inventing a story like this. It's too circumstantial."

"Well, what is the story?"

"I'll have to condense it," Jane said, looking at her watch for the second time, "I'll be late for my appointment, as it is."

"And I'm due at the theatre pretty soon, so condensed will suit us both."

"Well, about six months ago Anne's father became very ill. At least, that's what everyone was told, although his complaint was never exactly specified and he didn't have an operation or anything; but Anne put it around that he was on his deathbed and she started going up to spend the night with him in London once or twice a month."

"I was aware of that and anyone who understood the first thing about her doom ridden imagination would find it entirely plausible."

"All right, here's the garnish: One night, after this had been going on for several months, there she is in London, sitting at her father's bedside, waiting for the angels to gather him and, lo and behold, she's not doing anything of the kind. She's dining with a pretty young man in a restaurant off the Charing Cross Road. Tom was taking a client out to dinner and he happened to choose the same one. Anne didn't see him at first, so engrossed was she, but she passed right by his table when she left, so naturally she had to stop and say good evening and she introduced the young man as her brother."

"She hasn't got a brother," I said, forgetting myself.

"Precisely, darling! Although Tom didn't know that at the time. He simply assumed, as one would, that the

99

reason they were together, and looking so haunted, was because of their father's illness. In fact, he never gave it another thought until about three months later."

"When Cath happened to pass the remark that Anne was brotherless?"

"No, it was Harry who gave the show away. He was telling Tom how chuffed they both were about the pregnancy and what a splendid thing that Lizzie wouldn't be an only child and so on. He said that he and Anne had both suffered from that. Take the present case, he said, with her father so ill and all the burden of it falling on her. So then Tom became very disturbed to think of his old friend being deceived in this way and he told Cath the story and asked for her advice."

"Which was the next best thing to shouting the news through a megaphone from the roof of Storhampton Town Hall."

"No, that's unfair, because in fact her advice was to keep quiet. It wasn't until Anne lost the baby that she decided it couldn't make matters any worse and might actually be beneficial for Harry to learn the truth. Furthermore, she came up with what I consider to be a rather charitable explanation."

"That'll be the day!"

"She said it might account for Anne's obsession about the baby being a boy. In other words, she hadn't been unfaithful in the conventional sense, but knowing how passionately Harry wanted a son, she'd deliberately picked on a man whose wife, let's say, had already given birth to a couple of healthy males, believing that this would up the chances by at least fifty per cent. And you know something, Tessa? I wouldn't be a bit surprised if she were right. It's just the kind of batty thing Anne would do. And now I really must fly. I don't want to get on the wrong side of this gentleman before we've even started. We'll be in enough trouble, as it is, the way Charles is carrying on. Bye, Tessa. Take care, and good luck with the play!''

Looking the way she did, it was inconceivable that the stoniest legal heart in the business would not turn to butter the minute she stepped into the office and, as it happened, there were still at least two outstanding questions I would like to have put to her; but I could tell that her mind had already moved on to her personal concerns and that it would be hopeless to try and detain her. So I paid the bill, which she had been in too much of a hurry to glance at, and then wandered over towards the lifts in a rather abstracted frame of mind.

It had been my intention to go directly to the main exit and pick up a taxi, but at the last minute I changed course and set off towards the florist department, meaning to order some flowers for Anne. My route took me through the main hall, which was how I happened to catch sight of Jane yet again. She was seated in one of the green leather armchairs, which faced each other in two rows down the entire length of this marbled salon, and was so deep in conversation with her next door neighbour that neither of them noticed me. This may have been just as well, since the man beside her was Harry.

CHAPTER TWELVE

"And what would your other questions have been, if you'd had a chance to slip them in?" Toby asked.

This was on Friday, soon after my arrival in the country. Anne had left the hospital two days earlier, but apart from a brief telephone call to satisfy myself that she was making good progress, no contact had been established with Braithwaite House and I had spent my first evening bringing Toby up to date with all the news and, in particular, with my long and informative conversation with Jane. He likes to keep pace with current events, so long as no personal intervention is required on his part.

"One of them has already been answered," I replied. "I was dying to know whether in fact it had cheered Harry to learn that his precious new baby belonged to someone else."

"And the answer?"

"Judging by his expression when he was talking to that deceitful redhead, I should guess that it was about the best news he'd ever had in his life."

"Unless he didn't believe a word of it, recognised it from a mile off as an innocent little gambit of Cath's to rock the boat and tip Anne overboard?"

"In that case, he should have been sitting at the bedside, not waltzing around London on clandestine assignations with Jane Nicholson."

"You may be doing him an injustice. I like to take the charitable view once in a while and they could have met there by chance. Numerous people do pop in and out of that shop for one reason or another."

"There was no question of popping in and out this time. They looked set for the afternoon. And she was the one who was supposed to be in such a tearing hurry to keep an appointment with her solicitor. No, there's no excuse for either of them. I consider they are behaving disgracefully."

"And do you also consider there is any truth at all in that charming little story Cath came trotting out with so opportunely?"

"None whatever. I know Anne too well for that. She has her weaknesses, poor girl, but she is steady as a rock where Harry is concerned. Unfortunately, though, one can't just dismiss it as invention on Cath's part. It would follow that she had got round Tom to back her up and somehow, snake though he is, I don't think he'd stoop as low as that. Or rather, I do, but not for her sake. He and Jane might have concocted it between them, I suppose, since it now appears that she also has a vested interest in discrediting Anne, but I can't see Tom and Cath working as a team. He obviously dislikes her and is probably jealous of the influence she still has over Harry."

"You almost make it sound as though he were in love with Harry himself?"

"Well, perhaps he is, in a way. Not in the sense you're suggesting, but I do think he's dazzled by all that culture and breeding. It's a great feather in the cap of a man who's so pitifully conscious of his own humble origins to be the chosen friend of one of the local nobs, even a run down one like Harry. Of course there's the land too, and the money he was hoping to make by going into partnership with Harry, but he must have plenty of other financial fish to fry as well as that, so I can't believe it's the main attraction."

"And you think the story was pure invention, to drive a wedge between Harry and Anne, either for his own sake or for Jane's?"

"Or maybe blew up some trifling little incident into a big sensation. And then, having carefully worked out the dates, passed it over to Cath, confident that she would snatch the first opportunity to spread it around in the right quarter."

"And what would your second question have been?"

"I was wondering whether anyone had bothered to warn Anne about these tales that are being circulated so freely. Presumably, she was strapped to her hospital bed, having blood transfusions, when the story broke, so she may not even be aware yet of her new reputation. Oh well, I may be able to find that out when I see her to-morrow. I'm afraid it means you'll be on your own here, at the mercy of the telephone, for quite a while, because there are a number of items on the agenda and it's bound to take time to work through them."

"How tiresome! I'm not sure that I care for my furniture spending so much time in other people's drawing rooms."

"It can't matter to you if I go in the afternoon. If I were here, you would only be upstairs in your room, pretending to be hard at work but actually having a snooze. Besides, I bet you're just as curious as I am to find out more about that funny business with the goat."

"Wrong on both counts! No one could be as curious as you are, and goats don't fascinate me in the slightest."

"But, honestly, Toby, don't you find it rather puzzling? I mean, why should that dim old party suddenly take to creeping up on people and butting them in the back?"

"You imply that there was some human agency involved?"

"I don't know, but I'm mad keen to hear Anne's

version of the affair. That's for starters, but there's something else as well. I haven't told you this yet, but when I spoke to her last week, before the miscarriage, she mentioned that there'd been another attempt to do her in."

"Oh, really? What a charmed life she leads!"

"Except that it was actually aimed at the child, and not the mother, that description hardly applies. Unfortunately, she wouldn't give me any details on the telephone. Scared that someone might be listening, I gather."

"And that's your full programme for to-morrow afternoon?"

"It's all I can think of at the moment."

"Oh well, it could be worse, I suppose. It appears to boil down to this : was it Cath, or Mary, or the goat who butted her in the back? Does she know that she has been unfaithful to Harry? And what happened just before that, which she was too frightened to speak about on the telephone? You ought to be able to get through that lot in a couple of hours, and then you can come straight back here and give me all the answers over the teacups."

CHAPTER THIRTEEN

In picking the early afternoon as the most propitious time to call on Anne, I was influenced not so much by thoughts of Toby's welfare as by the chance it would provide of finding her alone, and Lizzie safely despatched on her afternoon walk.

Apart from the inhibitions which were bound to be aroused by Harry's assertion that Lizzie was fully capable of following every word of an adult conversation, there was also Anne's ferocious and over-developed maternal instinct to be reckoned with. It was virtually impossible to conduct a coherent conversation when she was breaking off every other minute to jump about or scream, either because Lizzie was teetering on the back of an armchair and about to overbalance and plunge to her death, or because Anne had suddenly become convinced that she had formed the resolve to do so.

I therefore set forth immediately after lunch, although, due to unforseen circumstances, did not reach my destination until some forty minutes later; the circumstances being that on the way I met the Nicholsons.

They were on a blackberry picking expedition, he hooking down the higher branches and more luscious fruit with the handle of a walking stick, while she daintily gathered in the harvest and dropped it into a pudding basin which he held in his other hand.

We chatted for a while, extolling the beauty of the day and the delights of blackberry and apple pie and Mrs Nicholson then informed me that I should find Jane at the swimming pool, where indeed she had taken to spending most of her afternoons, and suggested that I should join her there.

Not that any of this delayed me for long, for it was quite evident that they were only being civil, without having the slightest wish to detain me and it struck me as I walked away that one reason why their company was so dull, and yet so oddly soothing, was that they liked each other immensely and were totally self-sufficient. As an extension of this idea, I began to wonder if Jane might also often feel herself to be the odd man out of the family and that this, despite the inevitable friction it caused, perversely inspired her to come tumbling home to the parental roof when her marriage came unstuck, out of a sub-conscious wish to break up their tight little enclave. In other words, she was just as much a victim of other people's married bliss as Harry had been, and if her parents had welcomed her with open arms, as an alleviation to the tedium of their hum-drum existence, she might have stayed away. But then again she might not, and at this point in my reflections, finding the combination of plodding uphill and wrestling with an entirely new train of thought rather too much to take in the same stride, I sat down to chew a blade of grass and consider the matter thoroughly.

Ever since coming upon Harry and Jane, seated side by side in the London store, it had been depressingly clear to me that there was more to this than even the whacking great lot which met the eye. Given Harry's well-known susceptibility to the female sex, plus the fact that Jane, in addition to being a raving beauty, was now delicately poised for the rebound, plus also the fact that Anne was temporarily hors de combat, it was not to be wondered at if they had indulged in a little light flirtation, or even if matters had gone a good deal further than that. The bothering part was that it should have reached such a high emotional pitch in so short a time, and I had now begun to view the situation from the directly opposite standpoint. How would it be, I asked myself, if their falling for each other had been the cause and not the result of Jane's marriage going on the rocks? Obviously, in that case, the affair could not have developed very fast or furiously while she remained in London, and was it for this reason that she had descended with all speed on Hollings Farm?

However, I next reasoned, even such propinquity as that would not have sufficed for long, so Tom's help had been enlisted and he had obligingly given things another boost by providing her with a job. From this point they had been but a step away from insinuating Jane into the Braithwaite household, where, in Toby's terminology, she had rapidly transformed herself into part of the furniture.

I was quite pleased with this assessment, which seemed to cover most of the points and there was a corollary to it as well. Before Harry hit on his bright idea of drawing Tom into the web, he may well have been designing a future pattern of regular coming and going between his own house and the Nicholsons; but naturally it would have been suspect to have singled them out for such attentions, to the exclusion of everyone else. Therefore, various other families had to be bombarded with invitations too. I had always been conscious of a flaw in the argument which depicted him as hell bent on ingratiating himself with his neighbours in order to melt their opposition to his building plans, for it did not accord with his arrogant, self-indulgent nature to go canvassing for approval for his behaviour. The only department of life where he bothered to put himself out was the petticoat one and it was far easier to believe that it was Jane, rather than the new houses on Platt's Meadow, whom Toby had to thank for his recent popularity.

In theory, of course, there was nothing to prevent Harry exchanging Anne for Jane, but obviously it would have been a tricky business to deliver a blow of that force to a woman who was about to bear him a son, still more so perhaps to one who had recently been deprived of that privilege, through no fault of her own. In any case, I did not believe that any idea of substitution had entered his mind. Even if he could bring himself to give up Anne, there was still Lizzie to be considered and I doubted if anything would induce either of them to part with her.

My final conclusion was that he would endeavour by every means in his power to hang on to what he had got and simply add Jane to the collection. It remained to be seen which, if either of them, he would now decide to marry.

These deliberations having delayed me by some twenty minutes, I did not arrive at Braithwaite House until getting on for three o'clock, a misdemeanour for which I was querulously hauled over the coals by my hostess. She was lying on the drawing room sofa, looking so drawn, ill and unhappy that I felt constrained to turn the other cheek.

"Sorry, very sorry," I said meekly, "but I didn't realise there was any particular hurry."

"Then you ought to have realised," she said, still very petulant, "I've been lying here for over an hour, waiting for you to come, and I get so dreadfully bored and depressed when I'm left on my own. I was beginning to feel quite suicidal."

"Then I really am sorry, Anne, but why are you all on your own? Isn't Harry around?"

"No, he's not. He's gone to London to see his publisher. That's always happening now, about the third time in two weeks, and I think it's a bloody scandal. Why the hell can't the rotten publisher come down here and see him, if it's all that important? Harry was awfully worried about leaving me, but I told him that you'd be spending the afternoon here, so he really hadn't any excuse not to go."

"If I'd known that, I'd have taken care to be punctual, but you didn't tell me."

"Oh well, never mind, let's not waste any more time arguing about it. I've got loads to tell you."

"Good! Start at the beginning!"

Inevitably, practically all of it centred round her miscarriage, subsequent suffering and present mental anguish, although she could add nothing to what Jane had already told me concerning its onset; simply that she had been leaning up against the fence, balancing Lizzie on her hip and then, out of the blue, this sharp and painful blow in the back.

"But only one?" I asked at this point, "it didn't go for you a second time?"

"Didn't have to. Once was enough to knock me flat and drop Lizzie at the same time. That was the real hellish part, because I was so petrified that the beastly, vicious old mare would kick her or trample on her before I could get there."

"And when you finally picked yourself up, what was the goat doing?"

"How would I know? That was the last thing that interested me. I couldn't care less what it was doing."

"You didn't happen to notice if it was still close by or had moved away by then?"

"No, I didn't. I have a vague recollection of its being somewhere around, but no more than that and I really can't see why you're going on about it so. What could it possibly matter what the bloody thing was doing, after it had knocked me down?"

So, having exasperated her enough for one afternoon, I allowed her to continue the story in her own fashion and at least, by this means, one of my questions was answered without my having to find a way to ask it. There could be no doubt, once I had heard her own version of Harry's reaction to the catastrophe, that the news of her infidelity, as concocted by Cath and Tom, with or without some help from Jane, had not yet reached her. This gave reason to hope that Harry no more believed it than I did.

"And the really miserable thing," Anne went on, "almost the worst part of all, is that my gynaecologist has put the thumbs down on starting another for at least two years. I feel I've let Harry down so badly."

"Never mind," I told her, "in two years you'll still be young enough to have six more, if you want them; and in the meantime you've got Lizzie. Where is she, by the way?"

"Out with Jane, of course. I told you that."

"Are you sure?"

"Yes, of course I'm sure. Jane came to fetch her over an hour ago. That's what made it such a bore when you didn't turn up."

"You mean, she's taken her down to the pool?"

"No, I don't mean anything of the kind. Honestly, Tessa, you are in a peculiar mood to-day. Jane wouldn't dream of taking her to the pool, she knows how I feel about it. They've gone for a walk on the Common. We agreed that the woods are getting much too dark and damp now and I certainly don't want her to go anywhere near those beastly animals, whatever else."

Perhaps I should have let it pass. No doubt, Lizzie would have turned up safe and sound at the appointed time and Anne would not have been any the wiser; but

I was infuriated by Jane's duplicity and the urge to spike her guns proved too strong.

"She may have agreed to all that, but I should tell you, Anne, that Jane is at the pool this afternoon. I have it on the best authority."

Having spoken, I was instantly dismayed to see a look of absolute terror come into her eyes. The blood drained away from her face and for a moment or two she was literally incapable of speech.

"Is it true?" she then asked in a whisper.

I nodded.

"How do you know?"

"Her mother told me. On my way up here."

Anne pointed to the telephone: "Ring up, Tessa! Find out if they're there!"

Her voice had regained a little strength, but she still seemed half paralysed by fear and I was regretting my rash words more and more.

"Oh, but is that really necessary? Jane's perfectly capable of seeing that she doesn't fall in or anything. She wouldn't let her drown, if that's what you're afraid of."

"For God's sake, don't joke about it! You don't understand . . . I've got this ghastly premonition . . . Ring them up!"

"Okay, if you insist. What's the number?"

"Six five eight."

I dialled it and listened while it rang and rang. Anne had not moved off the sofa, but she was sitting bolt upright and she never took her eyes off me for an instant, while we both waited in silence.

"No answer," I said, replacing the receiver at last, "but nothing to be alarmed about there. You probably can't hear the telephone out on the terrace and, as I told you, her parents aren't at home; they're getting the blackberries for dinner. Now, do try not to worry, love! I'm positive there's no need for it."

I might just as well have spoken in Chinese, because she continued to stare at me with a vacant expression, saying flatly:

"Listen, Tessa, please don't say any more; you've got to get down to Hollings right away, this very minute. If Lizzie's there, bring her back, or get Jane to drive back, anything you like, but just go, will you?"

"Oh, all right, if it means so much to you, but I do assure you that she's in no danger whatever."

Once again, she ignored all arguments and reassurances, probably did not even bother to listen to them.

"I'd go myself, only I'm still pretty shaky and you'd be so much quicker."

"Of course you mustn't go yourself. That would be even more nonsensical."

"I could, you know, and I will too, if you don't get a move on. I can't explain, but I just feel it's most terribly urgent to get there at once. I beg you, Tessa!"

There was no more to be said and I did as she asked, promising to telephone from the farm, but reminding her that she would have to contain herself in patience for at least twenty minutes.

In fact, this was a slight underestimate because, although I set off with a good semblance of speed, I allowed the pace to slacken as soon as I was within sight of the footpath to Hollings Farm. The conviction grew stronger with every step that this time Anne really had overdone it. She had always been neurotic, up to a point, about Lizzie's safety, but the miscarriage and its attendant miseries must have pushed her temporarily beyond that point, for, with no question at all, she had genuinely been in a state of terror on learning of the child's whereabouts. I was prepared to put on a show of humouring her, but not to wear myself to a rag by galloping through the countryside on a warm afternoon on such an idiotic mission.

The house was deserted and the terrace too, although there were some damp towels lying around, to show that the pool had recently been used. I conscientiously walked to the edge and peered down through the clear turquoise blue water, but was not surprised to see no little corpse lying on the tiles at the bottom.

It hardly seemed worth while telephoning Anne to pass on such a negative report and, in any case, it was reasonable to believe that she was now re-united with her cherished Lizzie and all fears forgotten. However, having given my word, I felt obliged, for form's sake, to carry it through to the letter and dutifully dialled the Braithwaite House number.

As I had half expected, there was no reply and, resisting the temptation to indulge in a brief, cooling splash, I compromised with a few minutes' rest on a chintzy chaise longue, before setting forth once again on my weary way up the hill.

Jane's car was parked half way up the drive, which it had not been before, and when I was within a few yards of the house, she came round from the other side of it. Mary was with her and it was she who was pushing the pram.

They stood chatting for a moment or two, and then Mary sprinted off back in the direction they had come from, towards the grass walk leading to the copse. Grasping the pram handle and looking very decorous and saintly, Jane wheeled it over to the cedar tree and sat down on the bench, where she was in full view of the drawing room and Anne's bedroom.

If they had shouted it through a megaphone, they

could not have proclaimed the truth more plainly and here was the full extent of Jane's perfidy finally revealed. I felt deeply aggrieved, more for myself at that moment than for Anne. I could not tell how often Jane had played this shabby trick of taking Lizzie from her mother, then handing her over to Mary at some pre-arranged spot and tripping off to follow her own devices until it was time to repeat the process in reverse; I could not tell and I did not care. I only knew that I had been shoved around quite enough for one afternoon and I turned on my heel and marched off, yet again, down towards the valley and home.

It was an impulse I was later to regret, for if I had battled on into the last round, I might, just conceivably, have been instrumental in saving Anne's life.

CHAPTER FOURTEEN

There was hindsight in those last words, and perhaps also a slight bias in favour of my own intuitive powers, for these would have needed to be at their keenest for it to have made any real difference. Otherwise, if I had gone back into the house and found the sofa bare, so to speak, I should have concluded, somewhat as Jane did half an hour later, that Anne had observed the charming tableau in the garden and so, with no further use for my services, had retired with a heart at peace to her bedroom.

Only one person's presence might have altered the course of events and this was lacking, for, whether or not Harry had really been with his publisher on his two previous absences, it was certainly true of this one. The meeting had lasted from three o'clock until half past four and it was nearly six before he arrived home.

Before this, there had been a number of developments, starting with Jane's activities soon after my own departure, which were as follows:

The instant Lizzie awoke from her nap, Jane had taken her out of the pram and carried her into the drawing room. There was no one there, but as her allotted time was not quite up, she had resigned herself to wait, patiently at first, but with increasing resentment as the minutes went by and Anne still did not appear.

At five o'clock, which was well into overtime, she had gone upstairs to investigate. The bedroom door was shut and, repeated knocks having brought no response, she went downstairs again and telephoned the cottage. Cath had answered and when the situation had been explained to her she said that it was highly inconvenient for her to leave at five seconds' notice, but that she would come over as soon as she could manage it. In the meantime, she had urged Jane to desist from further attempts to rouse Anne, who had most likely taken a sleeping pill, as she was all too prone to do nowadays, instead of trying to pull herself together, and that it could be highly dangerous to wake her from a drugged sleep.

Around half an hour later she and Mary had arrived together, Mary in tearful and mutinous sulks because she had been forced to stay indoors and tidy up her bedroom, instead of going for a ride on the pony. Jane had thankfully turned Lizzie over to them and retired from the fray.

The situation had then turned static again, but orderly too, because, to give her her due, Cath was eminently capable of looking after a two-year-old child, specially with a television set in her armoury, without any of the alarums and hysteria which went into Anne's performance.

She was on the point of taking Lizzie upstairs for her bath when Harry returned. He had no compunction whatever about waking someone forcibly from a drugged sleep, maintaining, on the contrary, that it was probably the most useful service one could perform for them, but he was unable to put it into practice because when he went into Anne's bedroom she was not there.

However, there was still no panic, for at this moment Cath recollected, as if by magic, that Anne had telephoned her just after lunch and had mentioned among other things, that I would be spending the afternoon with her. It now became crystal clear that the silly girl must have misunderstood the arrangement and that, in fact, I had collected her in Tony's car and taken her back to his house for tea. Then, of course, we had been chatting away, as we always did, and had forgotten the time. No cause for alarm whatever.

While not precisely alarmed, Harry stuck to the view that, no matter what else Anne might forget, it would not be Lizzie's bedtime, and he thought it more likely that she had been taken ill. He therefore telephoned me to ask if this were so, but with inevitable results.

Thus, through a combination of duplicity, vacillation and inertia, Anne's life slowly ebbed away.

CHAPTER FIFTEEN

It was generally agreed that the verdict would be "Suicide While the Balance of the Mind was Disturbed", and indeed the deep depression she had been in at the time, combined with the physical circumstances of her death, almost precluded any alternative; almost, in my opinion, but not entirely.

On the face of it, everything was perfectly straightforward, but there were one or two anomalies which, however trivial and insignificant they might appear to an outsider such as Inspector Mackenzie, who was in charge of the case, must have struck any close acquaintance as curious, to say the least.

In the first place, instead of Harry's abortive telephone call to me being the signal for a search party to be organised forthwith, as had happened after Lizzie's disappearance, he seemed to have meekly fallen in with Cath's suggestion that less drastic measures should be tried first. These had included ringing up all their friends in the locality and even Anne's father in London, but all with negative results, Mary in the meantime having taken it upon herself to go on foot to the village and make enquiries of Mrs Chalmers.

As a consequence, twilight was rapidly turning to darkness before the search proper began and even then Cath had attempted to stave it off by suggesting that they should wait for Mary's return, despite the fact that even a half-wit would have realised that the chances of Anne having either visited Mrs Chalmers or confided in her in any way at all were so remote as to be safely ruled out.

It was only with the arrival of Tom and Jane that matters took a more sensible turn. They had naturally been among the first to be approached and, being together on the terrace when the call came through, had received the news via Mrs Nicholson, together with her personal opinion that Anne had gone out for some fresh air and, being still so weak, had fallen down and injured herself.

This, as it happened, was a repetition of the view I had already put forward myself, but for some reason it did not find favour with Harry until Tom and Jane appeared in person to urge it upon him, and only then was the remedy decided on. Torches and first aid equipment were rounded up and the four of them set forth, Cath having hastily volunteered to stay behind and guard Lizzie.

It was Tom who found her and this provided another small mystery because, by rights, it should have been Harry. Considering that it was the very place from which another missing relative had recently been so expeditiously retrieved, he might have been expected to make straight for the pavilion. He justified the omission later by saying that he had in fact approached it, but finding it shut up and in darkness and knowing all about her claustrophobia in general and her strong dislike of the place in particular, had not wasted time by going inside.

As a matter of fact, I found this explanation reasonable enough, for the mere fact that Anne had indeed gone in there, apparently of her own accord, was far and away the most puzzling aspect of the whole affair. Up to a point, there was something to be said for the opposing argument, put forward at the inquest, which maintained that if, as appeared unmistakeable, she had been contemplating suicide, she would certainly have been in an abnormal state of mind and, furthermore, even a full

cylinder of gas would have been inadequate for the purpose if she had left the door open, but I was still not
convinced.

In any case, no such thoughts as this influenced Tom,
who, finding both sections of the door unbolted, opened
the top half and shone his torch round the interior until
it came to rest on Anne, huddled face downwards at the
bottom of the spiral staircase. Whereupon he had pulled
the whole door as wide as it would go and, pausing only
to turn and shout for Harry before tying a handkerchief
round his nose and mouth, had dived inside, gathered
her up and brought her into the fresh air.

There was nothing heroic in this conduct, apart from
the risk it entailed of getting dust and cobwebs on his
whipcord trousers, for the whole business was accomplished in less than a minute, and the flow of fresh air
which had preceded him through the open door had
already done something to cleanse the atmosphere. Nevertheless, even those few seconds were enough to make him
feel unpleasantly groggy and when he had been joined by
Harry and they found that Anne was dead, it did not
take them long to establish the cause, beyond all doubt,
nor to verify that both taps on the gas cylinder had been
turned up to their fullest extent.

All the same, Mrs Nicholson's guess and my own had
been partly right, since, although she had died from
suffocation, the post mortem revealed that her left ankle
had indeed been broken.

This, to my way of thinking, was one of the oddest
features of all. No satisfactory explanation was put forward to account for it, either then or later, although the
official view was that, having made all the necessary
arrangements to end her life, she had attempted to climb
to the upper storey, so as to die in comfort on the camp
bed, but had stumbled and lost her footing in the dark.

The jury accepted this reasoning as entirely plausible and, since none of them had either met Anne or possessed the vaguest insight into her character, perhaps I should not blame them. The real shock arose from the discovery that those who had been closest to her in life also appeared to find it credible.

Personally, I was not to be budged from the conviction that, if the balance of the mind had still been sufficiently undisturbed for her to consider her own comfort in that situation, then nothing on earth would have induced her voluntarily to go into the pavilion in the first place.

CHAPTER SIXTEEN

Thanks to a heavy rehearsal schedule, I was excused from attending the inquest, but, on the assumption that I had been the last person to see Anne alive, was required to make a statement in advance, to be read out in court. My interrogator was Detective Inspector Mackenzie, of the Storhampton C.I.D., an old acquaintance, though not one whom I had hoped would never be forgot.

Unlike Tom, he made no pretence of failing to recognise me, which was rather a bad omen and, following Robin's advice, I played safe and stuck to the bare facts, carefully avoiding comments or opinions.

Obviously unprepared for this, he was somewhat at a loss and made several attempts to trick and tempt me into indiscretions, all but one of which I managed to parry. The single exception was unavoidable because it required a straight answer and it came right at the end.

Having twice pressed me to say whether I had anything, however trivial, to add to my testimony and twice been told that I had not, he then formally solicited my opinion as to whether the deceased had been in a suicidal mood when I parted from her, to which I again replied with a firm negative.

This was more like it and, for the first time, he was able to assume his disapproving, bitten up look and to ask me whether I fully understood what I was saying.

"I believe so. 'No' is one of those fairly simple words and I hadn't realised it was open to several interpretations."

"I am suggesting, you understand, that your opinion

on this point might be called unique. You do realise that it is not shared by any of the other witnesses who have been interrogated?"

"No."

"No?"

"Not having been present during their interrogations, I could have no idea what their opinions are."

He sighed, laying aside his cold and empty pipe, a sure sign of being disappointed by the way things were going. Perhaps as a child he had had a dummy stuffed in his mouth whenever he squeaked, because he was deeply attached to this pipe, which had evidently become the symbol of contentment and self-confidence. In that mood he would waste endless time lighting and re-lighting it, appearing to lose interest in the subject under discussion while he gazed in perplexity at the bowl, and extinguishing his match with the gesture of one waving farewell to an ocean liner. It was most distracting and I was relieved to find that his confidence was still too shaky for this brand of mental torture.

"Would you care to tell me then, Mrs Price, what yours is based on? I presume we are dealing in facts, not airy fairy conjecture or feminine intuition?" he added hopefully.

"Only one fact, but I hope it will be enough. The reason why I left Mrs Purveyance when I did was because she had particularly asked me to go to Hollings Farm and make sure her little girl had not fallen in the swimming pool."

"Was there any reason why she should have?"

"None that I know of."

"And don't you consider that showed her to be in an abnormal state of mind?"

"I can't say whether it did or not. To do so would border on airy fairy conjecture, I suppose. My point is that, abnormal or not, it did not denote the mental condition of one intent on suicide. How could it have mattered what became of the child, if she was soon to be beyond knowing or caring?"

"Had it occurred to you that she may have had quite a different motive for sending you off on an errand which you admit yourself was unnecessary?"

"No. What sort of motive had you in mind?"

"For instance, that she was anxious to get rid of you, by any means she could find, in order to leave the coast clear to carry out her plan of self-destruction?"

I was slightly shaken by this question and must have betrayed the fact in some way, for he unclasped his hands, which had been locked under his chin and allowed one of them to fiddle lovingly with the stem of his pipe.

"No," I said, retreating to my former position.

"Why not?"

"You can call this intuition, if you want to, but I swear on oath that her anxiety was genuine. It's true that she had been nervy and depressed before, but her attitude changed quite violently when she learnt that Jane . . . Mrs Ewart, that is, had taken Lizzie to the swimming pool. She had always been obsessed by the fear of some harm coming to the child and she became absolutely terrified."

"But you do admit that she had been depressed beforehand?"

"Yes, although I wouldn't have said abnormally so, in the circumstances."

"And that is all you can tell us?"

"Yes, I'm afraid it is."

"So we can only assume," the Inspector said, casting a last sorrowful look at the pipe, "that after you left she either had some kind of brain-storm, or else, let us say, with time to reflect on it, she began to regret having sent you on this errand and to see the absurdity of it. Does that strike you as plausible?"

"Could be. She was rather volàtile. Up and down, you know."

"Thank you, I had taken your meaning. And, if that were so, is it not also possible that as a result, she began to fear she might be going insane and that while in the grip of this mood she made up her mind to end her life? Or have you any other suggestions to account for what happened?"

As a matter of fact, I had plenty, but I stuck to my guns and my denials and had the satisfaction of seeing him tuck the cold and empty pipe into his pocket, before standing up to shake my hand and thank me for being so co-operative.

"Nothing much wrong with that, is there?" Robin asked, "I don't find any major flaws in his reasoning, although I gather from your expression that you do?"

"Certainly I do. It is all based on the premise that Anne committed suicide."

"Oh, I see! And you don't go along with that? Well, perhaps I ought to warn you about that old saw that people who threaten suicide are not those who put it into practice. Contrary to popular belief, they very often do."

"I know that. I haven't been married to you for all these years without picking up a few tips; and I'm not pretending that Anne was incapable of such a thing, specially when she was in the lowest depths of ill health and depression. All I'm saying is that she didn't do it."

"I see! And you don't recognise any contradiction in those two positions?"

"No, because in the first place the method absolutely rules it out. She was terrified of confined spaces and terrified of the dark. I'll now throw an old truism back at you, which is that people arranging their suicides invariably go to great pains to make it as cosy for themselves as they can; pillows in the gas oven and all that kind of thing. Anne, more than most, was strongly addicted to the fleshpots and on no account, no matter how distraught, would she have elected to spend her last hours in a place she detested so much."

"You can't say how people would behave in such extremities of despair. To do so would be to put yourself in their minds, which even you might admit is impossible."

"Oh, very well. I still think I'm right, but since there's no way of proving it I won't insist. I have another reason for regarding Inspector Mackenzie's theory as a load of old bosh."

"Which is?"

"His contention that what finally drove her to do it was her belief that she was going round the bend."

"What's wrong with that? It can be quite a powerful incentive, particularly when it happens to be true."

"Oh, I grant you that she was slightly dotty in some ways, but the point is that she didn't know she was, and this obsessive anxiety about Lizzie was nothing new. She'd always had it and no one had ever got within miles of convincing her that it was in any way neurotic. So why, suddenly out of the blue and off her own bat, would she have begun to equate it with insanity? Of course she wouldn't."

"Why didn't you tell him so?"

"Well, honestly, Robin! Weren't you the one who warned me to deal in facts and nothing but the facts?"

"Yes, but it could be argued that Anne's overprotective, overdeveloped maternal instinct came into that category."

"It wouldn't have helped if I had told him. He'd only have taken it as further evidence that she was out of her mind. He's absolutely set on proving it was suicide."

"One can see why. Everything does point to that, despite your objections."

"I simply find it rather strange, if not sinister, that someone should have died in that way after a series of accidents which she herself believed were attempts on her life. While she was alive, I was prepared to write them off as coincidence, or maybe figments of her own imagination, but not any more. There was nothing imaginary about the last one."

"And yet it is hard to see how anyone could have enticed her into the pavilion. And what would he or she have done next? Said 'Oh, excuse me a minute while I turn on the gas' and then walked out and shut the door while Anne stood meekly by? She hadn't been knocked unconscious, you know, or the contusions would have shown up in the post mortem."

"She had broken her ankle, though. She could have fainted."

"Yes, that's true," Robin said thoughtfully, "I admit it hadn't occurred to me, but I suppose it is conceivable that she fell and broke her ankle in the wood and was carried into the pavilion in a faint. Unlikely, but conceivable."

"What's so unlikely about it?"

"Mainly the fact that she should have been capering about in the wood at all, when she ought to have been at home, hanging on your return."

"I have a theory to account for that too," I told him. "Quite a neat one, in my opinion. Want to hear?"

"Why not? Your theories often contain a few piquant touches and I daresay this one will be well up to scratch."

"Ironically enough, it was good old Mac the Pipe who first gave me the idea. He said that after I left Anne to go searching for Lizzie at the pool she would have been all on her own in the house and that's when she must have gone plunging into the darkest depths of despair and decided to end it all. Well, I don't in the very least agree with his sequence, but it is true that, so far as we know, she certainly was alone during that forty or fifty minutes and yet something must have happened because it's the absolutely crucial period."

"And you have guessed what it was?"

"I may have. You see, obviously, her anxiety wouldn't have subsided after I left; on the contrary, it would probably have increased with every moment that passed and it would have been quite natural for her to have become restless and to have started moving around to various vantage points, hoping to catch sight of me. If so, she may well have gone into the library, which, as you know, overlooks the grass walk up to the copse, in the hope that I would be coming back that way. As a matter of fact, I didn't because, although it's slightly shorter, it's also a lot steeper and I was getting a bit fatigued by then. But Anne was never one to be over-concerned about other people's comfort and convenience, so it would have been quite a logical position for her to have taken up. And it would also explain why she didn't hear the telephone when I tried to call her from the farm. There's no extension in the library, in case it should disturb Harry when he's working."

"So?"

"Well, cast your mind back to the scene at the actual moment of my return. I have come along the drive, passing Jane's car on the way, and I am standing at the corner of the house, with a view over the lawn to the cedar tree. So I'm in a first rate position to observe Jane and Mary when they pop round from the far side, complete with pram. They would have been invisible at that point to anyone in the drawing room or Anne's bedroom, in one of which they fondly imagined her to be closeted with me. But supposing she had, in fact, been in the library then, staring hungrily out of the window, and had witnessed their arrival even before I did? What would her reaction have been to that?"

"She would not have been best pleased, it is safe to say that. I rather visualise her as screaming the roof off."

"Do you? I'm not so sure. My picture is of her being temporarily stunned; so bemused at first that she doesn't properly take it in. She didn't particularly like Jane, but she trusted her implicitly where Lizzie was concerned and I am sure it would have taken her a minute or two to realise how she had been duped. By the time the horrid truth had burst upon her Mary would have been trotting along, halfway back to the copse, and this is where we come to the crux. If I'm right so far, it would be understandable if Anne still weren't behaving very rationally and I should guess that for the moment all her rage would have been concentrated on that deceitful girl, scampering off so smugly and getting away with it. So what happens? Forgetting how weak she is, she goes barging out by the french window and sets off in hot pursuit. The intention being to catch up with Mary, confront her with her crime and promise that the news will be passed on to Harry the instant he returns from London."

"And then what?"

"Well, rather an anti-climax, really. Instead of catching up with Mary and giving her hell, she trips over a tree root, breaks her ankle and passes out."

"Whereupon Mary, who knew she was being chased, goes back to find out what has become of her pursuer, sees Anne lying unconscious on the ground, carries her into the pavilion and so on and so on. Is that the idea?"

"I suppose if anyone did that, it is most likely to have been Mary. She was within close range and I think Anne always believed she was the one who was out for her blood. Furthermore, she must have had a very guilty conscience, old Mary, and fear could have driven her to desperation. The snag is that I don't understand why she should have gone back at all. Surely, once she realised Anne was losing ground and hadn't a hope of catching up, the wise thing would have been to bolt on home and then swear she hadn't been out of doors the whole afternoon? Her mother would have backed her up against Anne any old day, and between them they could have used it to chalk up another black mark against her. In other words, she had become so demented that she was suffering from delusions of persecution."

Robin said: "But Mary is not very wise and if Anne had cried out when she fell, she might have turned back instinctively. Perhaps it was only when she found her pursuer at her mercy, so to speak, that the idea popped into her head to rig up this suicide?"

"Well, I am glad to find that you are taking my theory so seriously, Robin. Personally, I wouldn't have credited Mary with the ability to think that fast, but it may well be the answer. On the other hand, there's no denying that lots of other people had the opportunity. Cath could have been out collecting free fire wood. Harry could have returned from London and, finding no female companionship on tap in his own house, set out to seek some at the cottage. No, that won't do because, if he had arrived home then, he would have seen Jane in the garden and would undoubtedly have stopped to dally with her, before going indoors. Wrong again! How do we know Jane was sitting in the garden at all? We only have her word for it and she could have seen Anne run out of the house and have guessed what was afoot, in which case she'd have had no compunction in leaving her post and joining in the chase. So, if Harry had come back and found no one around except Lizzie, he'd have been curious, to say the least, and probably gone looking for them all."

"Leaving Lizzie to her own devices?"

"On the contrary. I'm sure he would have hauled her out of the pram and taken her along. Then nothing to stop him dumping her on the ground or handing her over to Jane, while he carried Mummie into the pavilion for a nice long rest. He says Lizzie understands everything that goes on, but I expect he also feels he can rely on her discretion in certain matters. So it could have been Harry, it could have been Jane, or the pair of them working as a team."

"You've left out Tom."

"And that will never do, because he must certainly be included. He has the run of the place, free to come and go exactly as he chooses, and he could easily have come across Anne while he was out in the wood, popping off rabbits, or whatever it is."

"And that's the lot?"

"Well, I suppose if we are being absolutely scrupulous we shall have to include the Nicholsons."

"Are you serious?"

"No, not really, but I threw them in to show you what a wide field Inspector Mackenzie would have to operate in, if he were wide awake enough to consider an alternative to suicide. I was observing them with half an eye while I sat on the grass, doing my meditating, and they were certainly moving round the field in the right direction. At the rate they were going, they would just about have reached the edge of the copse at the appropriate time. Still, that would be for him to worry about. As I say, I don't seriously believe the Nicholsons were involved. They're much too considerate and well mannered to commit murder. And they couldn't possibly have had any grudge against Anne. She was their best safeguard in the matter of the new houses, which would have ruined their view as much as anyone's. I should think that would far outweigh any faint hopes they may have had for getting shot of Jane by marrying her off to Harry, which as far as I can see would be their only motive."

"And Harry?"

"I don't seriously believe it of him either. He adored Anne and would have been incapable of harming her, even though she may not have fulfilled all his many requirements when she was pregnant and out of sorts. No, if I were the Inspector and if I were treating this as murder, my money would be on Mary to win, with Cath, Jane and Tom in a photo finish for the places."

"And, if you were he, how would you set about proving it?"

"That's the tricky part, isn't it? I suppose one way might be to begin by asking each of them in turn what they were up to when they were seen prowling round the pavilion at four thirty-five on the afternoon in question."

"There you are, then!" Robin said. "Theres' one more reason for being grateful that you're not Inspector Mackenzie."

CHAPTER SEVENTEEN

Not being Inspector Mackenzie, the best I could do was to begin by asking her what had become of the goat.

We were seated in opposite corners of the 8.32 to Paddington and she looked quite strange and incomplete without her pink knitting. The train had already trundled through Ealing Broadway, so there were only ten minutes left, and all I had gleaned from her thus far was that she was on her way to London to buy herself something to wear at the funeral, though why this should be I could not tell, for I could scarcely recall seeing her in a single garment which would have looked out of place at such a function.

However, I concluded that she had probably complained to Harry that she had nothing suitable to wear and he had responded by pressing some fivers into her hand and driving her to the station, and that she was now stuck with it. In any case, it had not been a fruitful line of enquiry and I had made several attempts to draw her out on more interesting topics, although all with equal lack of success.

Having met on the Storhampton platform, we could hardly have made for separate compartments when the train eventually pulled in, but almost from the moment of embarkation she had barricaded herself behind *The Daily Telegraph* and resisted all efforts to divert her attention away from it. Only now, when it was time to put away her spectacles, to smooth her gloves and tear her return ticket in half, was she forced to lay down her shield, and she answered flatly :

"Nothing, so far as I know. Why do you ask?"

"You mean you're keeping it? I don't see how one could bear to do that."

"Why ever not? She's only nine years old. That's no age for a goat."

"I didn't mean that. I was thinking that seeing her every time you looked out of your window would bring such horrible reminders. After all, she was the direct cause of Anne's miscarriage, so I suppose it would not be an exaggeration to say that she was indirectly responsible for her death?"

"I don't wish to sound callous," Cath said, forgetting that people invariably do sound callous when they are being callous, "but life must go on, you know. These things happen and it's very sad that they should, but they mustn't be allowed to govern the lives of us poor unfortunates who are left to pick up the pieces. I'm very attached to my old Elsa and if I got rid of her I should only have to buy another, so where's the sense in that? Besides, if you ask me, she had no more to do with Anne's miscarriage than you or I had."

This being one subject on which I was prepared to ask as much as she could take, I said, not too eagerly:

"Oh, really? But surely it resulted from her being butted in the back and then falling over and being so frightened for Lizzie? At any rate, that's what they told me."

"Oh, I don't doubt it. It was Anne's own version of the affair, but I'm not entirely convinced. If you ask me, it was all in her imagination."

"Honestly? And yet she did fall over and she did drop Lizzie and something must have caused it?"

"Perhaps the mare came too close and Lizzie wriggled, so that Anne lost her balance and they both went down. Who can say? We'll never know the real answer, but in all the years I've had her Elsa has never behaved viciously before and when I went out to see what was up, there was the poor old girl grazing away quite peacefully and not taking a blind bit of notice of anyone. If you ask me, we should be a little bit wary of laying the blame on her."

The train was slowing down as it passed through the deserted hinterland of Royal Oak and, considering it time to change course, I said :

"I suppose you'll have to buy Mary a new outfit too, won't you?"

She was staring out of the window, one hand gripping the wooden ledge, as though bracing herself for the swift escape, but everything conspired against her. The train stopped dead, about fifty yards short of the platform, to allow an express to come past in the other direction and in the lull which followed before we inched forward again, I repeated my question.

"No," she replied, adopting, from necessity, a normal upright position, "there's no need. Mary won't be coming to the funeral."

"Really? Why's that?"

"Because I don't consider it would be good for her. She's very highly strung and emotional and I don't want her to be more upset than she need be."

"No, I suppose one wouldn't. So she'll be able to stay behind and look after Lizzie while it's going on?"

"On the contrary," Cath said, as the platform slid slowly past us, "we've arranged for her to go back to that friend of Jane's in Essex for a few weeks. She was quite happy there and making herself useful, and Harry and I both feel that she should get right away into a more healthy atmosphere during this difficult time."

"Can I drop you anywhere?" I asked, as we jostled along the platform, for I was agog to find out what lay behind this urgent need to bundle Mary out of the way, and why it was that her nerves had all at once become too fragile to support her through the funeral service of a hated rival, "I have to take a taxi because of this lumbering great suitcase."

It had been a forlorn hope and I was not greatly disappointed when Cath muttered something about getting a bus along Oxford Street, meanwhile taking advantage of the slowing down effects of my suitcase to hurtle through the barrier ahead of me and become lost in the crowd. It was not one of my more successful encounters, but I did not see the journey as entirely wasted.

CHAPTER EIGHTEEN

Ironically enough, Anne's funeral did not take place on a matinée day and I was able to attend.

"I thought you loathed and dreaded such occasions," Robin said when I told him of my plans.

"So I do and I'm not looking forward to it one bit, but I was her oldest friend, you know, and at least Toby has promised to support me."

"If you can call that support!"

"Better than nothing and, besides, there's some unfinished business to tidy up, if I'm not to be nagged by it for the rest of my days."

"And you hope to accomplish that at a funeral?"

"Something may turn up. People have been known to betray themselves when they are under great emotional stress."

"I call that wildly optimistic; but perhaps the kind of emotional stress you have in mind is remorse? In that case, it is rather unfortunate that Mary won't be present since, according to you, she would be carrying the biggest share of it."

"Well, exactly, Robin! And the fact that she has been packed off to Essex does make one wonder if others have the same idea. Doesn't it suggest that at least one of them has something to conceal which they are afraid of Mary blurting out, even if it only points to her own guilt?"

"Only?"

"Alternatively, that she knows something which points to someone else's guilt, and that makes it even more intriguing."

"Well, I wish you luck, and you can certainly do with some. Will you be taking the car?"

"Yes, if you don't need it?"

"No, and I rather wish you didn't either. I think it might be as well to drop the business now and try and put it out of your mind."

"I was her oldest friend," I reminded him again.

In the end Toby was unable to keep his promise to accompany me because at the last minute he was struck down by food poisoning, or diphtheria or something, I forget the exact details and was temporarily confined to his room. He did not miss much, for the service was even more depressing than I had anticipated, macabre being the only word to describe it.

The Vicar diplomatically referred to the deceased throughout as 'our sister, Anne', which may have made Harry feel a bit like Bluebeard, but at least she was surrounded by her siblings in death. Her identity was still further eroded by Harry and Cath occupying the front pew and looking the very picture of conjugal solemnity. The sight of them reminded me to find out from Jane whether the divorce had been called off, or was going through despite the fact that the chief beneficiary, as it were, was no longer with us. If not, it would presumably now be necessary for Cath to pull another trump card out of her pack, if she were to keep her house and view intact.

Jane was in the pew behind them, with her parents and Tom, and in the one behind that there were two men, one young, the other middle-aged, sitting a little apart from each other. I found this puzzling on several counts because the elder of the two was Mr Monk, Anne's father.

There was plenty of room in their pew, so I went in

and sat on the end nearest to him. He recognised me immediately and placed one hand over mine, when I rested it on the pew in front. I noticed that his own was thin and heavily veined, that his jacket was several sizes too big for him and that in appearance generally he had aged about twenty years in as many months.

I was sorry for this, but in one respect not entirely displeased to find him so sadly altered, for at least it vindicated Anne and gave the lie to Tom's malicious gossip. As I had believed all along, he clearly had been seriously ill, though possibly her own imagination had furnished the trimmings, convincing her that the complaint was a terminal one, without hope of even a partial recovery.

Nevertheless, he was evidently still in very poor health, unable to stand and kneel with the rest of us, frequently putting up a hand to shield his eyes, in a gesture which spoke of fatigue as well as grief, and it soon began to dawn on me that she might not have exaggerated so very much, after all. Furthermore, the young man on his other side, despite the gap between them, was obviously acquainted with him and could perhaps have been a nurse, or attendant of some kind, not there for personal reasons but in a professional capacity.

That supposition was strengthened by the care and solicitude with which he offered his arm to Mr Monk when the service was over and by their slow, laborious progress down the aisle, in the wake of the rest of the congregation.

However, the relationship was not so impersonal as I had imagined, for when they emerged on to the gravel path outside, where I was waiting, he introduced the young man as his godson.

Before this, though, I had been greeted with demonstrative and tearful affection by Harry and in a restrained and ladylike fashion by Cath, who then graciously, and in a very proprietory manner, invited me up to the house to join in the wake. Not wishing to commit myself, I gave a vague answer, saying that I might do so for a moment, but that I was in a hurry to get back to London, which was not strictly true.

I judged the young man to be about thirty, although thin dark hair already receding from a high domed forehead made him at first glance look older than this. His name was Miles Stevenson and Mr Monk explained that the dear, kind fellow had travelled all the way from the Persian Gulf to be with him at this sad time. Having dutifully applauded the gesture, I asked whether they would be going up to Braithwaite House and he said he rather thought not. Harry had very kindly suggested it, but he was feeling a little tired and, since he did not know any of Anne's friends in the neighbourhood, was bound to feel out of place.

He spoke in a quiet, subdued voice, but I was relieved to find that in spite of his evident frailty and the ordeal he had just been through, he was perfectly coherent and in command of himself. Nevertheless, I was staggered to hear him add a moment later that another reason for not putting in an appearance was that they had a taxi waiting to take them back to the station.

"You can't mean you came down by train?"

"Why not?" he asked smiling. "They still exist, you know, whatever you may have heard to the contrary."

"Oh yes, I know that; I was thinking how tiring and uncomfortable it must have been for you."

"No, not too bad at all. It is not much more than an hour to Paddington and I live quite close by, in Bayswater, as I'm sure you remember."

Miles, who had stationed himself a few feet away

from us, as though reluctant to intrude, now intervened, stepping forward as he said :

"It is all my fault. I only got in rather late yesterday and there wasn't time to arrange anything about hiring a car; but please don't worry, Mrs Price, I'll take very good care of him."

"I'm not worried," I told them, "not in the least, because I positively insist on giving you a lift. It's no trouble at all, since I have to go straight back to London, in any case, and the Bayswater Road is on my route."

The offer was accepted immediately and without argument and any self-sacrifice it entailed was quickly offset by the look of relief on both their faces. There had been a tiny sacrifice though, because from the corner of my eye I had caught sight of Jane and Tom returning together from the graveside. They were on their own, so presumably the ceremony was not yet over, and if ever two people looked as though they were cooking something up it was they. I could not entirely repress a twinge of regret that my impulsive gesture had so effectively denied me the chance to find out what it was.

"You don't look like an oil man," I remarked, "but I suppose you must be?"

We were five miles out of Storhampton and I could see in my rear mirror that Mr Monk had now closed his eyes and, from the look of him, had either died or fallen asleep. He had chosen the back seat, on the grounds that he would be more comfortable with his legs up and we had covered them with a rug and rigged up a pillow for his head.

Miles had performed his part with admirable deftness and had then installed himself in the front seat where, as though to underline that quality of aloofness which I had noticed in him already, he sat rather stiffly, and in a way to leave as wide a gap between us as possible. However, silence always makes me uneasy, particularly my own, and rather than continue it all the way to London, I was prepared to risk offending him by discoursing on any subject which came to mind.

Fortunately, his reserve seemed to stem from dislike of physical contact, rather than the verbal variety, for he answered in a tone of mild amusement:

"Why don't I look like an oil man?"

"Too pale and intellectual, for a start. I always visualise people in that job as burly, hard drinking types, with red faces and hairy hands."

"Where did you get that idea from? The movies?"

"Mainly."

"Well, they're not all like that, I can assure you."

"As you are here to demonstrate?"

"No, you mustn't take me as typical either. I happen to be employed by an oil company, but I have nothing to do with the product. It's the personnel who are my concern."

"Oh, I see! You sort out their stresses and strains, their housing and marital problems?"

"Not even that. Something more mundane, you might say. I'm a doctor."

"Yes, of course," I agreed, wondering why I hadn't already guessed.

"So I measure up to that image, at least? Or did it come from the movies, too?"

"Mainly, although, like most people, I have run across one or two in real life, as well."

"And what is distinctive about them?"

"Curiously enough, they often tend to look rather unhealthy. Still, I suppose it's understandable, in your case, if you spend most of your time immured in an air-conditioned surgery and only go out of doors after sunset."

"I have also just spent a considerable time immured in an air-conditioned aeroplane and have about sixteen hours' sleep to make up, so you mustn't be too hard on me."

"No, I was forgetting that. And what a break for your godfather that you were able to come! Will you be staying on for a bit?"

"Unfortunately not. I've already used up my home leave for this year. I can only manage a week at the outside."

"Do you enjoy your life there?"

"In some ways."

"That doesn't sound very enthusiastic. Did you go from choice, or did it just happen? I hope you don't mind my asking all these questions?"

"Not at all, it's rather refreshing. Makes a nice change from people who either aren't remotely interested, or else try to find things out without asking questions."

Despite the compliment, it looked as though my own approach was no more likely to bring results, for he had turned his head to look out of the window and remained in that position, apparently spellbound by the vista of Northholt aerodrome. However, when we had circled one more roundabout he returned to the subject, saying:

"It was a combination of the two, really. I was restless, on the look out for any excuse to leave England, and this offer just happened to come along. On the whole, I'm lucky that it has turned out to be as rewarding as it has."

"You're not married?"

"Oh God, no. If that day ever comes, I'll pack it in or ask for a transfer. It's no place for the little woman. That was one of the things that most appealed to me, in the mood I was in."

"Oh, I see!"

"Do you?" he asked doubtfully.

"I was thinking that perhaps oil rigs in the Persian Gulf may be the modern equivalent of shooting tigers in Africa. You know, the thing that strong silent heroes used to do when the love of their life had scooted with the garrulous cad."

"Not so far out," he admitted, and was about to enlarge on this, I believe, when we were interrupted by a faint and muffled groan from the back seat.

"You all right, Sir?" he asked, instantly swivelling round and giving his full attention to the patient. There was no response, nor was the sound repeated and a few minutes later Miles reverted to his former position, saying:

"He's okay, I think. Just a bad dream, or maybe a little spasm of pain. He seems to have dropped off again now."

However, the thread had been broken and I had been brought back to more immediate concerns:

"So you must have known Anne quite well too?" I asked him.

"Oh yes. That's to say, my sister and I used to see a lot of her when we were children; not so much in recent years."

"All the same, her death must have been a terrible shock?"

"Well, yes and no," he replied, after some consideration.

"Honestly? You mean you weren't all that surprised?"

"Not altogether, no. Naturally, it came as an appalling shock when I first heard the news. These things always do when they actually happen, however much one may believe one is half prepared for them."

"And you were half prepared for this?"

148

"I think I must have been. Somewhere at the back of my mind I suppose I had always expected it might happen. She was a loser, you know; one of those people who are constantly defeated by life, and, let's face it, in some respects her own worst enemy. She was always talking about suicide, even as an adolescent. I know that was done partly to impress and that it's not supposed to have any significance, but in my experience it very often does."

"My husband would agree with you."

He did not ask whether my own experience had brought me to the same conclusion, but continued thoughtfully:

"If you really want to know, it was the manner of her death which came as the worst shock. That I was not in any way prepared for."

Here I was in full agreement and eager to learn whether his objections to this small detail mirrored my own.

"I wouldn't call it a detail," he replied. "You were at school with her and you must know how unlike her it was to choose that way out? And it isn't as though she had no choice; there were other means available and she suffered dreadfully from claustrophobia. It is the thing I remember most vividly about our nursery games. In fact, I think it may well have dated from that period. There was one occasion, I remember, when she got shut in the cupboard and my naughty sister pretended she'd lost the key. Poor Anne was unconscious by the time we brought her out from sheer terror."

All this was most interesting and informative and, for the first time, the answers to some of the riddles surrounding Anne's death began to take shape in my mind. Hoping to hear more, I dropped into the role of devil's advocate.

"I believe there was some reference in the inquest to

her well-known claustrophobia, but it was brushed aside on the grounds that there's no telling how people will behave when they're distracted out of their minds; and although you say she had other means to hand, it is difficult to see what they could have been."

"I don't agree at all," Miles said firmly.

"Why not?"

"Because it is my honest, and I may add, well founded belief that she had been contemplating suicide for some time and could, almost certainly did, provide herself with a weapon. Perhaps she would have hung on if the baby had lived, but once that hope was gone I daresay it was only a question of time. Still, there it is. It's done now and no use in dwelling on it."

"But why should the baby have made so much difference? I know that losing it was a hideous blow and naturally she was fearfully depressed, but it wasn't the end of the road. There was still time for her to have another; several, no doubt, if she'd wanted them."

"Oh well, she was an incurable pessimist, you know; always looked on the dark side and expected the worst. And most of it was so unnecessary. Take her father, for example! It almost broke her up when he became so ill, she was so desperately worried for him, but I really believe he is a much more stoical character than she ever gave him credit for."

This last observation hit me with such force that my concentration momentarily deserted me and, turning into a narrow street behind the Bayswater Road, I almost collided with a taxi, coming towards me in a bit of a hurry, past a line of parked cars on his left.

By an unlucky coincidence, this street was called Frederick Place and was the very one where Mr Monk had his flat, and either from a homing instinct or as a result of my slamming on the brakes so suddenly, he woke up, thereby ruling out any further discussion on this interesting topic. He thanked me very kindly for the lift, saying that it had been most agreeable and that he felt quite set up again after his little snooze.

I did not believe him, though. His eyes, when he said goodbye, reminded me of Anne's, dark and sad and curiously vulnerable; and in fact he died a few months later and I never saw him again.

I never saw Miles again either. He went back to the Persian Gulf and, as far as I know, is still there. Not that it made much difference, for I doubt if he would have spoken so freely had he not been physically and emotionally drained by a long journey, followed so quickly by the funeral of his childhood friend, a combination of circumstances which was unlikely to recur very frequently. In any case, as I realised later, he had already told me all I needed to know.

CHAPTER NINETEEN

The following Friday brought two developments, both momentous in their different ways and both taking the form of printed announcements. The first was that the notices went up in the theatre, confirming our worst fears. The play was to be withdrawn after a run of precisely eighteen days.

The second, which I did not see until I arrived home later that night, was a paragraph in *The Times*, referring to the forthcoming marriage of Mr Henry Purveyance to Mrs Jane Ewart, née Nicholson.

Robin, who had waited up for my return, pointed it out to me, hoping no doubt to raise my spirits after the crushing blow they had just received, and succeeding, furthermore.

"They're jumping the gun a bit, aren't they?" I asked him. "Surely the divorce can't be through already?"

"I shouldn't have thought so, but perhaps they wish to state their intentions publicly, so as to forestall any little move on Cath's part to back out of her promise."

"Although, presumably, that clause in the contract is still as binding as ever? She has to give him a divorce if he is to call off the battle for the new houses, so to that extent it is immaterial whom he marries. Except that, if I were her, I'd have preferred Anne to Jane any day. If you ask me, to coin a phrase, she's really going to be up against it when old Carrot Tops moves in, and the curious thing is . . ."

"What is the curious thing?" Robin asked, looking pleased with himself for having created the absorbing diversion.

"Simply that he wouldn't now be in a position to

marry Jane or anyone else, if it hadn't been for Anne. He told me that it was purely for her sake that he was making this deal with Cath, and I wonder why? I mean, why then and not before? Changing her name by deed poll must have shown him how humiliating she found her position, yet he doesn't seem to have made any attempt to alter it until just a few days before she died. Now do you suppose there could be a motive mixed up in that?"

"So you're sticking to your anti-suicide guns? Honestly, Tessa, no one could accuse you of being blown off course by every passing breeze."

"I realise that all the arguments exist to prove me wrong, but I still balk at the idea of her going all alone into that gloomy place and shutting herself up in the dark. It simply doesn't ring true and Miles, who knew her ages before I did, finds it equally incredible. I feel there has to be another answer and I'd just love to have one more stab at getting to it. Let's say it's for Lizzie's sake. I have a feeling she'll be in for quite enough trouble in her life, without the spectre of a neurotic, suicidal mother tacked on."

"If I were you, I'd tread carefully there. You might find yourself uncovering one or two things which would be still harder for her to live with."

"Which indicates that you also believe we haven't heard the full story yet? That's encouraging! Oh well, ring up Toby to-morrow, I daresay, and invite myself there for next weekend. Will you be free?"

"Doubt it. I'll do my best, though goodness knows what you hope to accomplish in one weekend."

"I could prolong it, if necessary, if anything at all promising were to turn up. I need hardly remind you that by this time next week, I'll have all the time in the world for digging and delving into matters of life and death, and anything else you care to name."

154

CHAPTER TWENTY

And, after all, I did not have to wait for the weekend before turning up a handful of earth because Jane, ever on the watch for a free hand-out, had noticed those fateful words, "Last Days", outside the theatre and she rang up on Tuesday morning to beg for two seats for the following day's matinée.

There was no question of refusing, or even of making it sound like a big favour because, judging on previous form, we should be playing to an audience of approximately thirty-five, about two thirds of it papered. Besides, I was ready to grab at any opportunity that came along to pry a little further into the affairs of Braithwaite House. So I told her that I would arrange matters with the box office and invited her to step round to my dressing room after the performance.

"Is Harry with you?" I asked, recalling with a pang of sorrow a dressing room scene in another London theatre, not so very long before, when I had asked Anne the identical question.

Curiously enough, the answer was not so dissimilar either.

"No, I brought my mama. She sent you her love, by the way, but she had to scoot back to the country. They've got some people coming to dinner. Poor old Harry is stuck at home, looking after Lizzie, believe it or not."

"Well, since poor old Harry happens to be poor old Lizzie's father, I don't find it all that shocking," I said, then realising that such priggishness would get me nowhere, hastily changed my tune and added thoughtfully:

"I've been wondering about that, though, Jane. Who exactly is going to have charge of Lizzie now? Obviously, Harry can't spend his whole life playing nursemaid."

"No, of course he can't. We're trying to get a full time Nannie, but it's not easy. Harry would prefer someone young and cheerful, for Lizzie's sake, but at the same time she has to be experienced and responsible enough to be left to it on her own, when necessary. That kind doesn't seem to be very thick on the ground and I have to tell you that it's not a job I'd personally strain any nerve to get. That kid's been so spoilt it's unbelievable. Anyway for the time being, Mrs Chalmers lends a hand when she's able to, and there's Cath too, of course, but it's all very hit and miss."

There was no hint in this of any affection on her own part for Lizzie, or of the slightest expectation of being called upon to look after her, even as a part time occupation, and the cynicism with which she had duped Anne, in her most vulnerable area, purely to further the business of stealing Harry from under her nose, was quite nauseating. If a further fillip had been needed to cement my determination to uncover the truth about Anne's death, this callous speech would have provided it. However, it was essential not to betray such emotions by a single word or inflexion and I strove to keep any touch of sarcasm out of my voice as I asked her:

"And you have Mary too, haven't you? Perhaps not the most cheerful or responsible girl who ever lived, but I presume she's only too happy to rally round and make herself useful?"

Jane made a certain amount of play with lighting her cigarette and then coasting round the room looking for an ashtray, although there was one within easy reach of her chair. She then said reflectively :

"That should be the solution, I agree. After all, their I.Q.s must be about on a par and Mary never tires of dressing dolls and tossing balls around, so she's ideal as far as that goes. She's also devoted to the kid, whatever delusions poor old Anne may have had on the subject. That kidnapping lark was just a storm in a teacup, you know. Admittedly, Mary behaved like a raving idiot, but there was never the slightest risk to Lizzie. Everyone knew that except Anne, and I daresay in her heart of hearts she knew it too and simply used it as an excuse to keep Mary at bay, because she was so neurotically jealous and possessive."

It had not escaped me that the whole trend of this speech had been to hammer home the point that Anne had been mildly insane, but I refused to be drawn, merely asking :

"So what's the problem, since Anne is no longer there to object? Don't tell me that Harry is respecting her wishes out of loyalty? That doesn't sound at all like him."

"Too right, darling! He's the least sentimental gentleman I've ever struck. It's one of the things I find so marvellous about him. No, oddly enough, it's Cath who's the fly in this ointment."

"You don't say! I'd have thought she'd be tickled to death to have Mary so harmlessly occupied?"

"Wouldn't you, though? But not a chance. She says Mary is still overboard about the suicide. It was all such a shock and she's a bundle of nerves and all the rest of it. Her point is that Mary would never deliberately neglect the infant, but she might do something silly while she's in this jittery state and it wouldn't be fair to load the responsibility on to her."

"And is it true? I mean about Mary being so knocked out by Anne's death that she can't function properly?"

"Yes, to be fair, I'd say there was more than a grain of truth in it. God knows why she, of all people, should be so cut up about it, but I have to admit that ever since she came back from Essex this time she's been acting very strange, even by her standards. Cath and Harry insist that she'll snap out of it, given time, but you know how they both have this blind spot about anyone in the family? Personally, I'd say they were being a trifle optimistic this time. The poor girl's obviously slightly round the bend."

"Really? What are the symptoms?"

"Symptoms is right. She complains of terrible head-aches and insomnia, for a start, and I must say she looks perfectly ghastly most of the time, all red-eyed and puffy."

"Anything else?"

"Well, jumpy, if you know what I mean? Drops everything she touches and howls like a dog if anyone breathes a word of criticism."

"Goodness me!" I said, having no need to simulate my profound interest in this sad report, which seemed to bear all the hallmarks of the guiltiest conscience north of the Thames, "that does sound pretty bad!"

"I agree, and I did make a faint effort to persuade Cath to have a word with Dr Bell, but nothing doing. Cath said she'd be worse still if we all started making a fuss and drawing attention to it. And Harry's just as bad. They both take the attitude that, if they ignore it, the nasty thing will go away. Well, that's fine, I suppose, but it's not all that easy to ignore someone when they go around casting such a deathly gloom, either having a nervous crisis, or sitting for hours staring into space."

Jane was certainly laying it on thick and I wondered

how many grains of salt should be added to this well cooked dish; though all for grabbing a second helping while it was going, I asked :

"Has she given up riding as well, then?"

"Oh, you bet! And refuses to set foot in the copse. That's understandable, I suppose, but after all, there are plenty of paths through it which don't go near the pavilion and, anyway, she can hardly avoid it for the rest of her life, can she?"

"She could, if they were to pull it down? Wouldn't that be best, from every point of view?"

"You'd think so, wouldn't you? I imagine most people would have razed it to the ground, by now; but then, you see, most people doesn't include Harry. He has these weird ideas and anything which either of his parents said, or did, or created is practically sacred. That dreary pavilion has been holy ground ever since his Dad sat up there at night, watching the birds and all that, and who the hell cares what came after?"

I recalled that Anne had also found this attitude difficult to live with, but did not consider it would be tactful to say so, and Jane went on thoughtfully :

"I daresay he might have grown out of it, you know, if Cath hadn't always been at his elbow, egging him on. The fact is, they approved of her; his mother probably picked her out for him to marry, so I suppose she felt she had a kind of duty to go on waving their flag for them after they died. Personally, I'm thankful to say that I never met either of them, so at least I won't have any hang-ups of that kind. With any luck, we'll be able to make a fresh start. Anyway, I must fly now, Tessa. Thanks for the tickets."

"Wait a minute, Jane! You've just reminded me that I haven't congratulated you yet. Have you fixed the date?"

"Oh Lord, no. It won't be for ages. We still have a hell of a lot to go through with our respective divorces."

"Really? You do surprise me!"

"Well, you haven't had any experience of it, lucky little you, but these things always drag on for months, you know. The lawyers see to that."

"I know that, you ass. I was only thinking that you must have made things even more complicated for yourselves by being so free with the news of your engagement. I realise that, so far as Cath and Harry are concerned, it's a mutual agreement and the collusion couldn't be more solid, so it won't make any difference there; but doesn't it give Charles a chance to gum up the works?"

"Oh, grow up, love! You don't honestly imagine I'd hand old Charlie boy a weapon like that, if he hadn't known all about it for ages? In fact, you could say," she added, looking over her shoulder as she opened the door, "that he forced our hands, in a way, by citing Harry as co-respondent."

So at least that guess had been correct and furthermore Jane had now come out with a real peach of a motive for the elimination of Anne and her widely publicised baby son. Unfortunately, I was unable to use it to bring Robin round to my cause, since no one could fail to see that it might also have provided Anne with a real peach of a motive for committing suicide.

CHAPTER TWENTY-ONE

"It was a rotten play," Toby said, "and you ought never to have touched it. I said so all along."

"It wasn't such a bad part," I protested, "and if I'm to turn down every play just because it's rotten, I'll end up as a very inexperienced, middle-aged actress. Anyway, why don't you occasionally get to work on one yourself, instead of this incessant carp, carp, carp?"

"As a matter of fact, I am seriously thinking of it. I have quite a good idea going at the moment. Incest, but treated in the lighter vein."

"Oh, that's nice, Toby! Do I play the comical sister, or the comical jealous fiancée?"

"Neither. This is the other variation; the girl who's in love with her father. You can play her, if you like."

"I'm not sure that I want to. It sounds dangerously like a rotten part in a rotten play."

"On the contrary, there are several amusing and original twists. You see, we have this girl who, as I say, is potty about her father and she sets out systematically to remove all the other women in his life, starting with her own mother, naturally."

"Murdering them, you mean?"

"Not necessarily. She tries a bit of that too, but makes a complete hash of it. In fact, all her schemes and machinations go hopelessly wrong. It's more of a farce, really, than what you might call high comedy. You see, this father is a great charmer and never short of female companionship and each time the daughter sets a trap for the reigning beauty she either falls into it herself, or a new reigning beauty bobs up to fill the void. What do you think of it, so far?"

"Not a lot. And what brought all this on, as though I needed to ask? You've been thinking of Mary Purveyance, I suppose?"

Toby sighed; "No, I haven't. That's the last thing anyone would do from choice. It's just that she forces herself on my attention. She has been pestering me and the only way I can endure it is by picturing her as a character in a play. I am sorry you don't think much of it."

"In what way has she been pestering you?"

"You won't believe this, but she wants me to give her a job."

"No, I don't. What sort of job? Mowing your lawn, or something?"

"I think I could have borne that more easily, although I can't say how Parkes would have taken it. He gets rather neurotic about his lawn mower falling into the wrong hands. No, she wants to do secretarial work, if you please! Typing and that sort of thing."

"And since when has she been able to type, let alone that sort of thing?"

"I know; it is a surprise, isn't it? But she assures me she has become quite proficient. Part of her duties with this poodle breeder was typing out pedigrees and diet sheets and so forth and she got the idea of using all her spare time to dash away on the machine. I gather the chief incentive was the prospect of spending long happy hours in Daddy's library, typing out his manuscripts."

"Then why has she come begging to you?"

"Presumably, she is under the illusion that in my line of business scripts are rolling off the conveyor belt every three or four weeks and I am out of my mind trying to catch up with the typing. Little does she know!"

"Quite so, but that wasn't the question. I meant why, if the aim is to work for her father, doesn't she do so and shut up? Why come to you?"

"Because Harry won't have any part of it, that's why. Or rather, I gather from the way Mary expressed herself, if you can so describe it, that his bride won't allow him to have any part of it. The poor girl is being pushed around more effectively than ever. That's what gave me the idea, you see? I thought how amusing it would be if she had murdered Anne simply in order to be number one with Harry, only to find herself up against a far tougher adversary. It's disappointing that you don't like it."

"I don't altogether dislike it, but I'll come back to that in a moment, because there's something I still haven't got the hang of. Why pick on you? I refuse to accept all that rubbish about you being so pushed for someone to do the typing. Mary may be retarded, but even she wouldn't be so silly as to believe that. So could it be that, having been eased out by Jane, she is now transferring her affections to you?"

"God forbid! What a perfectly shocking idea! I know I am old enough to be her father, but surely that is my only attraction? No, no, I think it is just that having been beaten in the first round, she has now set her sights on earning some money. Mine is the only house within walking distance which has a typewriter on the premises and she knows how softhearted I am. I feel sure that can be the only reason. I certainly hope so."

"What does she want money for? I mean, I do realise it's not all that unusual, but she has never needed it before. At least, if she did she simply asked Harry for a hand-out."

"Aren't you being rather slow? I've spent most of this long hot afternoon trying to explain to you that there have been changes in that household. Your poor deceased friend may have grumbled to you in private about the way things were done, but she seemed powerless to change it. Not so Mrs Ewart, née Nicholson. She would have no scruples about letting Cath and Mary starve before they got their hands on any more of Harry's money. In fact, she would probably take seats for it."

"Yes, I've got the point all right, but I still don't see Harry going along with it. His way would be to promise Jane anything under the sun and then walk through the woods to the cottage with a big fat cheque in his pocket. I feel sure Mary must have some other reason for holding back."

"Perhaps she is afraid he would want to know why she needed the money, and since the answer would most likely be that she is saving up for a new gas cylinder for the pavilion, or a sharp knife and a book on poisons, he might not be so generous. However, to be fair, I should tell you that the reason she gave me was that she wanted to get herself a room and a job in London."

"And also to be fair, that wouldn't be very popular with Harry either, so it could be true. Do you honestly believe that she shut Anne up in the pavilion and then turned the gas on?"

"Yes, of course. Don't you?"

"Yes. Which could account for the headaches and insomnia. Remorse, or more likely the fear of being found out, is wearing her down, and the object now is to get away to London and wait for the whole thing to be forgotten."

"That's not the way it goes in my play. I have her hell bent on collecting enough money to buy the tools to polish off Jane."

"And does she succeed? It might be helpful to know."

"Naturally, I haven't had time to work out the details

yet, but I imagine this is where we get the real swing to the farcical. Anyone as clumsy and inept as Mary could be relied upon to get it all mixed up, and this time I rather visualise the wrong person drinking the poison."

"That's interesting! I do hope it's Tom. But even so, I suppose it would still count as murder. The police would arrest her and take her away and that would be the end of it."

"No, not at all, nothing so crude. There is no apparent motive, you see, and no suspicion would fall on her. Furthermore, this father is very protective and, just to be on the safe side, he supplies her with an unassailable alibi."

"So how does it end?"

Toby sighed: "I haven't got as far as that and, in any case, you don't sound carried away by the plot so far. I'm not sure that I'll bother to work on the ending."

"Oh, but I think you should."

"Honestly? You're not just saying that to cheer me up?"

"No, I'm not. I think you should write out the synopsis, exactly as you've just told it, and then give it to Mary to type out and see what reaction you get."

"Yes, I daresay that would be highly amusing for you, but I'm afraid I can't oblige. She might come to the conclusion that I Knew Too Much and had to be Silenced, and I couldn't adsolutely depend on her to bungle that part of it."

"You could start by making it perfectly clear that I also Know Too Much. That would complicate the silencing and shoot up the chances of the bungle. We could even throw out a strong hint that Robin and the entire Metropolitan Police Force are in our team. How about that?"

"I am not quite happy about it," he admitted. "It is rather a big step to take. I shall have to think it over."

He was not given much time to do so, however, for within twenty-four hours Mary was dead and once again all the evidence pointed to suicide.

CHAPTER TWENTY-TWO

There were some minor gaps in the chronological accounts of her last hours, but surprisingly few contradictions. The gist, as stitched together by the various witnesses, was as follows :

According to Cath, Mary had got out of bed very early that morning, declaring later that she had lain awake since day break, and as soon as the sun was up had taken the dogs for a walk on the Common, in the opposite direction to the copse. Apparently, this had become something of a routine in the foregoing weeks and there was nothing particularly unusual either in the fact that she did not appear for breakfast at eight-thirty. However, she came back about half an hour after that, drank a cup of stewed tea and then caught the only bus of the day down to Storhampton.

She had refused to disclose the purpose of her journey, but at this point the story was taken up by Tom. He told the police that Mary had arrived at his office at approximately ten a.m. and demanded an interview. His secretary had been obliged to keep her waiting for over an hour because he was engaged with a client for the whole of that time. The suggestion that she would be well advised to call back later had been stonily ignored and it was after eleven when she was eventually shown into his private office, where she had promptly and without preamble, requested him to give her a job.

Not wishing to offend her and, presumably, wishing still less to offend Harry, who might have put her up to it, Tom had used all sorts of tactful dodges to head her off, starting with some tentative enquiries about her qualifications. However, this did not get him very far because the more he tried delicately to skate round the subject of her unsuitability the more stubbornly she insisted that she had become a highly efficient typist during her stay in Essex and, furthermore, that she was prepared to take any old menial job and to accept the minimum apprenticeship salary.

Tom had then pointed out that her only means of transport was a bicycle, which might do very well for coasting down to Storhampton in the morning, but was rather inadequate for the eight mile, uphill return trip in the evening. She had countered this by explaining that she intended to use the whole of her first week's salary for a deposit on a second-hand motor scooter and had then delivered the coup de grâce by reminding him that he had recently put someone even more amateurish than herself on the payroll, purely out of friendship, proceeding to press home this advantage by adding that she knew a very wicked secret about this particular person, which, if driven to it, she would have no hesitation on passing on to her father, thereby landing this person in very serious trouble.

In parenthesis, I was faintly astounded that Tom should have spoken so freely to the police of this little blackmail exercise, but Robin, who was my liaison with Inspector Mackenzie, explained that by a curious mischance most of it had been overheard by the secretary. She had entered the room while Mary was in full flood, to announce the arrival of another visitor, having no doubt been primed to do so at a given moment; but, unfortunately for Tom, there genuinely was another visitor, so instead of saying her piece and going away again, she ignored all signals and stood her ground until Mary's diatribe was concluded. By one of the odd coincidences which life is so full of, the new arrival was Mrs Jane Ewart.

She was still working for Tom on a commission basis and he had asked for her to be shown in immediately, perhaps preferring, in view of Mary's overwrought state, that the confrontation between her and Jane should take place in his presence, rather than in the outer office, with his secretary once again a witness.

As soon as Jane walked in, he had assured Mary that her application would receive his urgent attention and that he would do his utmost to accommodate her, but instead of accepting this as dismissal she had responded rather blankly by asking what time it was. On learning that it was past midday, all the spunk had gone out of her and, putting both hands to her head, as though to prevent it falling off, she had asked if she might have a glass of water and a short rest, to get her strength up for the return journey. It then transpired that, owing to her long wait, she had missed the only bus and would be obliged to walk home.

Naturally, the other two would not hear of this and it had ended, not without protest, in her accepting Jane's offer of a lift in the car. However, they had not set forth immediately, because Tom had suggested that Mary should wait outside for ten minutes, to enable himself and Jane to conclude their business, thus saving her another journey.

After this, they still did not go directly, either to the cottage or the big house, because Mary, who, according to Jane, had been very silent on the first part of the journey, had finally confessed that she was suffering from one of her splitting headaches. This had led to enquiries as to whether she was taking anything for them, to which Mary was reported as replying that she had tried aspirin, but they did not seem to do much good and her mother was not in favour of consulting Dr Bell, who would only prescribe a course of anti-biotics, which everyone knew were perfectly useless.

Jane gave this as her reason for making Hollings Farm her first destination, for she claimed to have felt indignant that poor Mary should be compelled to suffer in this way, just to gratify some prejudice of Cath's, and she knew that her mother had some marvellous migraine pills, which she absolutely swore by. Mary was ready to try anything and as soon as they reached the house Jane had disappeared into the bathroom, emerging shortly afterwards with four pills wrapped in a tissue, which she handed to Mary, recommending her to take one as soon as she got home and the others at four hourly intervals, if required.

She then drove the rest of the way to the cottage, waited in the car until Mary was safely indoors, and that was the last she had seen of her.

Taking up the story again, Cath said that she had not been at home when Mary returned because, after an early lunch, she had spent the whole afternoon at the Village Hall, sorting out clothes and marking them up with price tickets for a forthcoming jumble sale. Not unexpectedly, this was verified by half a dozen impeccable ladies who had been similarly occupied, but there was only her own word to account for her activities after six o'clock, when they all dispersed. The word was as follows :

Passing Braithwaite House on her way home, it had occurred to her that she might as well make herself useful by giving Lizzie her bath and putting her to bed. There appeared to be no one at home, but the garden door to the drawing room and kitchen was unlocked, indicating that the occupants were not far away, and she had sat down to while away the interval by watching a little television, a temptation she could rarely resist, Harry's set being so much superior to her own old fashioned little black and white one.

It was not until the programme ended that she realised she had been sitting there for a whole hour, and not until the following morning that she learnt that Lizzie had spent the night with Mrs Chalmers, Harry and Jane having arranged to dine out that evening. In fact, it appeared that Harry had been at home the whole time she was there, working in the library at the other end of the house.

She had returned to the cottage soon after half past seven and there found a note from Mary on the kitchen table, saying that she had gone to bed early and did not want any supper.

It was a chilly, overcast evening and so, using the letter as a spill, Cath had lighted the fire and settled down to spend it with her radio, her knitting and her boiled egg.

Mary did not appear the next morning and Cath concluded that she had again risen early and gone for a walk, though admitting to being somewhat puzzled by the fact that this time she had not taken the dogs. It was that circumstance, together with Mary's continued absence which, by nine o'clock gave rise to the first uneasiness, a sensation which became considerably more acute when she went upstairs to make her bed and noticed for the first time that the bottle of sleeping pills was missing from her bedside table. She had gone at once to Mary's room and immediately afterwards had telephoned, first to Dr Bell and then Harry.

However, there was nothing that either of them could do because by then Mary had been dead for several hours.

CHAPTER TWENTY-THREE

She had left no letter to explain this drastic action, perhaps in the belief that it would be superfluous, in view of some recent entries in her diary, which she had made no attempt to hide or destroy. There were three relevant passages and the first, recorded a few days after Anne's death, was as follows :

Oh God, what have I done now? How was I to know? Or in my heart of hearts did I know all along? I can't ever be sure. I can't ever trust myself again. God forgive me, for no one else will.

This was followed a few days later by :

Even Lizzie's eyes reproach me now. Does she know what happened? Will the truth come out when she learns to talk? Daddy says she understands everything and he's always right. I must keep away from her. If she doesn't see me, perhaps the memory will fade and be wiped out.

The last entry was the longest and had been written the day before her own death :

What am I to do? Time only makes it worse instead of better. I shall never wash away my guilt. Yesterday I thought I would go riding again. I wanted to ride and ride for hours, until I was worn out and so exhausted that I couldn't even think any more, but it was no good. When I went into the paddock and saw my beloved pony, my old true friend, I knew I could never get on his back again. What is to become of me? My life is ruined and it is all my own fault.

So it began to look as though Inspector Mackenzie had a second suicide on his hands, or alternatively, one

suicide and one murder, which at least would have the
virtue of cancelling each other out. However, a few
doubts crept into one mind, at any rate, when the results
of the autopsy came through. These showed that during
the hours immediately preceding her death Mary had
swallowed the equivalent of two migraine pills of the
type prescribed by Mrs Nicholson's London specialist,
the same amount of nembutal as was contained in one
tablet supplied to Cath by Dr Bell, plus a minute dose of
cyanide.

"There is a big question mark there," I said. "More than
one, in fact."

"You bet there is," Robin agreed. "Like how and
where did she get hold of that particular poison?"

"That's not what bothers me. I prefer to leave all that
plodding routine stuff to the police; going round all the
local chemists' shops, searching through the files to find
forged prescriptions and all the rest of it. What, in fact,
are they doing about it, incidentally?"

"More or less what you have credited them with.
They have also cast their net over a twelve mile radius of
the village where she was staying in Essex. Apparently,
she couldn't possibly have travelled further afield than
that. All of it, as you won't be surprised to hear, yielding
precisely nothing. They haven't turned up a whisker and
the lady with the poodles, whose premises have been
meticulously searched, can throw no light on it at all."

"As you rightly say, I'd have been surprised if it had
been otherwise, but what is the next move?"

"Well, the inquest has been adjourned, to give them
time to follow up their enquiries, as the saying goes, but
it is more or less a formality. The most popular theory
now is that Mary got her hands on the stuff through this
friend of hers in Oxford. She's not an undergraduate,

but she does appear to move around in a good many circles, including medical students. She also works as a doctor's receptionist, which sounds promising on the face of it, but no one is very confident of its bringing results."

"And then?"

"And then, I suppose, it will be up to the Coroner and jury to make what they can of it."

"Which is unlikely to come within miles of the truth and, in any case, my question marks don't refer to the cause of her death. I was thinking of those extracts from her diary."

"You are not suggesting they were forged, I hope?"

"Goodness no, nothing like that. I feel sure they were all her own work."

"What's the trouble, then?"

"I take it we're assuming that Mary killed herself out of guilt and remorse for having murdered Anne?"

"Well, to judge by her own words, she was chock full of guilt and remorse about something and that seems to be the most likely cause. Although, funnily enough, I do not get the impression that it was what they call 'wilful murder'."

"Neither do I."

"In which case, it's not too difficult to guess what might have happened, do you think?"

"I don't know, Robin. You tell me!"

"It's only a guess, mind, but I'd say that Mary was thrown into a state of hysterical terror when she realised that Anne had seen through the trick of switching Lizzie, and was giving chase. But then, as you've already pointed out, it is most likely that Anne tripped and broke her ankle and when Mary heard the scream she instinctively turned back and found her lying unconscious on the ground. So seizing this as a heaven sent reprieve, she bundles Anne into the pavilion and bolts the door. All the same, from the way she expressed herself, I honestly don't believe it was with intent to murder."

"Then why turn on the gas?"

"Yes, that is rather a contradiction, I agree, but perhaps it was intended as a kind of temporary anaesthetic? After all, Anne might have come round at any moment and if she'd started shrieking and bawling, as she most certainly would have, anyone might have heard her, and that would have put Mary in even deeper trouble. What she most needed was a breathing space and I daresay she thought the gas would serve the double purpose of providing that and of blurring Anne's recollection of the events leading up to her fall. At the very least, it would have made her less coherent about them, which in itself would have been to Mary's advantage."

"So you think she meant to go back almost immediately, to turn off the gas and open the door, to air the place out a bit before Anne was found?"

"Right, and also to make it appear that, no matter what she herself might subsequently claim, Anne had gone in there of her own accord, before the pain in her ankle caused her to faint. Yes, I do, and I also think she very quickly got the idea of saddling up the pony, so as to return to the pavilion on horseback and, having done what was necessary, cantering away at top speed, to set up an alibi for herself for the whole afternoon. But you'll remember that at this point her mother threw a spanner in the works by forcing her to go indoors and tidy up her bedroom. Then, after Jane had telephoned her S.O.S. they went over together to Braithwaite House, so there was still no chance for Mary to put things right at the pavilion. In fact, it must have been a terrible moment for her when they walked within a few yards of it, and that could well explain why she was in such a flat spin when they arrived. You agree?"

"With every word."

"I'm sorry, Tessa, this kind of exposition is usually your perogative, isn't it?"

"That's okay. I find it very informative."

"Well, I should warn you that there's worse to come, because I also think that if I'm right we have solved another small mystery."

"Which is that?"

"Why Mary was later so insistent about running down to find out if Mrs Chalmers had any news of Anne. You said at the time that it was ridiculous, because that was the last place she would have made for. I gather you saw it as just one more element in the general conspiracy to delay things, but I should say it was the reverse of that. Isn't it more likely that Mary was grabbing at any feeble excuse she could find to scuttle off to the pavilion on her own, before anyone else thought of going there?"

"Nevertheless, if that is where she went, how come that she still didn't turn the gas off and open the door?"

"Don't you think that might have been because she realised immediately that she was too late, so her only chance was to leave things exactly as they were, with the exception of the bolts, of course, and pray that it would be seen as suicide? In any case, I regard that as a rather niggling objection to my general theme and I am sure I can rely on you to punch a few bigger holes in it than that."

"You bet I can!"

"Right! Your turn now, then!"

"In the first place, Robin, you yourself very kindly drew my attention to one quite sizeable hole. It was when you suggested that everyone would assume that Anne had only fainted after going into the pavilion. It

177

reminded me that I once broke a bone in my foot and I assure you that it hardly hurt at all to begin with. In fact, I was certain that I had simply bruised it, and it wasn't until quite a bit later, when it had swelled up like a balloon, that the real, throbbing agony set in. So I think that rather disposes of the theory that, when Mary came galloping back to see what had happened, she found Anne lying out in the wood and already unconscious. However, I can see that you are not deeply impressed by that hole, and I admit it is the kind of thing which could vary with individual cases, so I will pass on to the diary."

"Ah yes, the diary! I gather you are not satisfied with it?"

"Not if your reconstruction is correct. For instance, she says that Lizzie's eyes reproach her. Now why the hell should that be? Lizzie was half a mile away, under the cedar tree, when all this took place, so how could she know anything about it? Harry says she understands everything, but I suppose even he would not credit her with second sight?"

"If you had recently murdered an innocent child's mother, whether intentionally or not, I think you might easily find yourself haunted by the illusion of the innocent child's eyes reproaching you. I know I should."

"Okay, but then why does she go on to say that if she keeps away from Lizzie, out of sight and out of mind, perhaps the memory will fade? What memory, for God's sake?"

"Yes, I admit that part is a little confusing, but you must allow that she was in a thoroughly confused state when she wrote it."

"Well, then there's the bit about her lovely old pony and how she can't bring herself to go anywhere near him, or climb on his back ever again. What on earth has he got to do with it? Innocent children may be all very well, but innocent ponies are quite another matter, and this one couldn't be linked with Anne in any way whatever. She hated riding and she was frightened to death of horses. The only time she forced herself to go near them was to amuse Lizzie by feeding them with sugar; firmly entrenched, I might add on the other side of the fence."

"Yes, and that brings us back to the strange behaviour of Elsa, the goat, doesn't it?"

"When everything started to go wrong."

"Leaving us with only one conclusion, would you say?" Robin asked, giving me a wary, speculative look.

"I'm afraid so."

"Had you guessed all along?"

"Good heavens, no. Don't tell me you had, Robin?"

"Well, let's say it occurred to me some while back as a possibility and, though several items didn't quite fit, nothing has happened subsequently to rule it right out."

"And you thought, if you bided your time, I might get there in the end? Honestly, how mean!"

"Well, I took the high road and you took the low road and yours was the harder one to travel. Which reminds me, do you think we ought to put poor Mackenzie out of his misery?"

"Tell him what really happened, you mean? I don't see why not. After all, he did light up the first beacon, without which my bumpy old road might have been even lower, so perhaps it would be only fair."

"I thought you said it was Miles, the young man at the funeral, who lighted your way?"

"He was a great help too, but it was really that old Mackenzie who got to the nub of the matter."

"Then I think you should be the one to tell him so,"

Robin said, "specially if you want him to keep his pipe in his pocket when we take him out to dinner."

One question continued to nag me, however, and later that evening I said:

"I am sorry to pester you about this, Robin, but if you suspected right from the beginning how, why and by whom Anne was killed, I do think you might have dropped a hint, instead of positively pushing me down all those false trails."

"Perhaps I was secretly hoping to be proved wrong and that one of your trails would finally turn out not to be false. After all," he reminded me, "she was your oldest friend."

CHAPTER TWENTY-FOUR

"Admittedly, this is pure conjecture," I said, when we rejoined Toby after a harmonious and blissfully pipe free evening at the Swan Hotel in Storhampton, "but it would never surprise me if you were the one who first put the idea into her head."

"Indeed?" he replied coldly. "When would that have been?"

"When they came to dinner here, just before she popped up in my dressing room and told me that someone was trying to kill her."

"I don't recall saying anything which could have started the downward slide."

"But you gave her a somewhat exaggerated account of my achievements in the amateur detective game and I daresay that was the seed from which this stunted oak grew."

"One might have expected it to be a deterrent, rather than otherwise?" Robin suggested.

"Perhaps it would have been with anyone else, but you see, having known me since I was about ten, Anne had no faith whatever in my abilities in that or any other department, so she never saw me as a serious threat. In fact, I bet she got a good deal of amusement out of stringing me along so prettily and outwitting me at every stage. She certainly fell about laughing when she was telling me I wasn't half so clever as I thought I was, and I daresay it was all that chat about murder which opened up those vast new horizons and pointed the way out of her problems."

"In that case, I apologise," Toby said, "I do recall the occasion now and a very tedious one it was. George Nicholson never opened his mouth, except to guffaw or shovel food into it and after dinner his wife coerced me into playing bridge."

"Well, that shouldn't have been too bad. Harry is a very good player, I've always heard."

"So he may be; too good for the rest of us, no doubt, because it was Anne who made up the four and she had even less idea of the game than you have. In fact, I had a nasty feeling that the whole thing was really engineered by Harry, so that he could sit on the sofa and gaze into the eyes of that red-headed nymphomaniac, and I do hate being manipulated, specially when there's sex involved."

"You mean you knew as far back as that that he fancied her?" I asked in amazement. "Honestly, people do seem to have been holding rather a lot back during these last few months."

"Well, I expect this is partly hindsight," he conceded graciously, "but I feel now that I was not so surprised as I ought to have been when you dropped your bombshell. It was the kind of situation one vaguely takes note of, without actually putting a name to it, which is perhaps just as well. The astonishing part is that the one person who never appeared to notice anything at all was Anne. Considering how jealous she was, I find that quite remarkable; and really, you know, Jane was a much more dangerous rival than either Cath or Mary."

"Yes, but the trouble was that she'd suffered so long from those two that she'd become obsessed by them. She simply couldn't see straight any more; and no escape from them either. I suppose she had a good chance of outliving Cath, but Mary would still have been around to dance at her funeral. Moreover, we all know that even the divorce wasn't going to change anything. Cath turned it into a weapon to entrench herself more firmly than ever. I am sure Anne was resigned to being stuck with them for eternity until she came to dinner with Toby and got this wonderful idea of killing off the pair of them and setting it up to look like suicide or accident."

"Though I still don't understand," Robin said, "why she had to complicate the issue by throwing out those hints and accusations that it was they who were trying to murder her. What did she expect to gain by that?"

"Well, I don't know either, Robin, and unfortunately I never had a chance to ask her; but she had a very lively imagination, you know. She almost lived on it, like meat and drink, and the more complicated a situation became the more she relished it. On the other hand, there may also have been a practical side. You could say two."

"Could you really?" Toby asked, "well, I think one will be enough."

"No, you had better have them both because they jog along quite nicely in harness. In the first place, she may have thought it a smart move to fabricate the existence of an unknown murderer whose target she was and in that way she would always have been able to claim that the wrong person had been stabbed, poisoned or gassed; that the intended victim had really been herself; and I'd be there to back her up every inch of the way."

"And in the end it was the wrong person," Toby remarked. "How very sad and ironical!"

"And the other practical side?" asked Robin, who likes to keep the record straight.

"It could have been a device to try out ideas on me, whereby she would dream up various methods of murdering someone, pretending they had already been tried on her, and I would point out all the flaws and demonstrate how they couldn't possibly have proved fatal and so on.

In that way, with my innocent but relatively expert collaboration, she would eventually devise the foolproof murder."

"Yet in the end she acted without any advice or guidance from you."

"True; but she'd tried out and rejected quite a few alternatives before that. Besides, look where it got her!"

"I shall never understand it," Toby complained, "imagine shutting herself up in that horrid pavilion when the gas was on! You both imply that that's what happened, so I must believe it, but it does seem rather forgetful."

"On the contrary, that's the last thing she had forgotten. In fact, her single reason for going in there at all was that she remembered it only too clearly."

"Then I must be getting old, for I can make no sense of it at all."

"It is really quite simple, Toby: just a question of timing, and I don't want to boast . . ."

"Oh, nonsense! Of course you want to boast. Everyone does. What you mean is that you don't want to sound conceited."

"Quite so; I don't want to sound conceited because it wouldn't be justified. It is Inspector Mackenzie who deserves all the credit."

"There is no need to go to the other extreme."

"Yes, there is, because among the questions he asked me was whether Anne could conceivably have sent me scurrying down to the pool for any reason other than the one she gave, which was to rescue Lizzie from drowning. I was so busy concentrating on hard facts and on not giving him the satisfaction of drawing me out that I might as well have been fast asleep. I answered with a flat negative and we passed on to the next question. It was only the bits in Mary's diary about Lizzie's reproachful eyes, and how she couldn't bring herself to go near the pony etcetera which cleared the mists and showed me how near the mark he had been."

"Then I certainly have nothing to boast about, for I don't see any connection at all."

"But the point is that she did have quite another reason for sending me to the pool, the soundest one of all. It was so that she could rescue Lizzie herself."

"Oh, a light dawns! I am being perfectly modest about it."

"She'd given Jane strict instructions not to go near the wood or the paddock, making the excuse that it was too damp under the trees and that their unpleasant experience with the goat had made the paddock forbidden territory. Her real reason was that, having by then made a telephone call to the cottage to check that Mary had gone out, she intended to belt down to the pavilion and turn on the gas. You'll remember, of course, that Mary was known to be spending all her waking hours in the little top room there, writing her memoirs and only going home to eat and sleep? The chances were that she had already taken herself off there, but even if things hadn't worked out according to plan, nothing would have been lost and no one would ever have connected a leaking gas cylinder with intent to murder. What she didn't know was that Mary's true destination that afternoon, as on so many, was a rendezvous with Jane, who was to hand Lizzie over to her. In fact," I added with mild dismay as the thought now occurred to me, "you could say that I was as much to blame as anyone for Anne's death. If I hadn't insisted so vehemently that Jane was at the swimming pool that afternoon, none of it would ever have happened."

"Does that count as boasting?" Toby asked.

"No, because I didn't realise what I had done. I

assumed that it was after I returned from the Farm and after she'd seen Jane and Mary coming back together that she ran down to the copse; but of course it wasn't so at all. By that time she was already lying in the pavilion, with a broken ankle, and the reason why she'd been in such an agony of impatience to get rid of me was simply that she had guessed straight away how she had been tricked and no doubt had visions of Mary and Lizzie playing peep bo together, with the door tight shut, so that no one would catch them at it, and the gas slowly leaking away downstairs. Every second's delay in getting there to rescue the child must have been a torment."

"Then why did it all turn out so differently?"

"Well, this is partly guesswork, what some people might dare to call airy fairy conjecture, but it's my opinion that they had never been near the pavilion and that Mary had broken still more rules by taking Lizzie to the paddock. How else to account for this phobia she later developed about the pony? He must have become associated in her mind with that terrible afternoon when her own sly deceit turned her into a murderess. What surely happened was that when she was on her way back to meet Jane, approaching, that is, from the opposite direction, she saw Anne go tearing into the pavilion. Naturally, with a guilty conscience like hers, she'd have been scared silly of the row that was in store for her and her instinctive reaction would have been to shut and bolt the door, leaving Anne incarcerated until such time as Lizzie had been restored to her official guardian and Mary had fixed herself up with an alibi for the afternoon. In other words, to saddle up the pony with all speed and pretend that she had been out riding. Unfortunately for that plan, her mother caught her in the act and we know what that led to. All the same, I daresay she wasn't badly worried at that stage. It was an alibi of sorts and we have to remember that she knew nothing whatever about the gas. Another thing she didn't know was that Anne, halfway up the staircase and plunged into pitch darkness when the door slammed shut, had broken her ankle and passed out. It wasn't until she and her mother arrived at Braithwaite House and found all the rumpus going on that she began to panic and that's why she hit on that apparently fatuous idea of going down to enquire at Mrs Chalmers."

"In fact, to tell Anne that the game was over and she could come home for tea now?"

"Only she was too late. If Anne wasn't already dead by that time, she must have been in such poor shape that Mary would have had a lot of explaining to do if she'd dragged her out and raised the alarm. And that's putting the kindest interpretation on it. For all we know, she may have been highly delighted, just for those few moments, by what she found. Anyway, she shut the door again and pretended to be as appalled as everyone else when Anne was eventually found."

"And later, she was awfully sorry, but . . . finding the guilt and remorse would not go away, swallowed a lethal dose?"

"No, nothing so straightforward. She was sorry all right, but everything indicates that her one great ambition was to put as much distance between herself and the pavilion as she could raise the money for. Being Mary, her sorrow was all for herself, not for the havoc she had caused; and it doesn't sound as though she had much to spare for Anne. Still, I suppose there's a thread of justice running through all this, because the cyanide was meant for Cath and it was planted, I need hardly say, by Anne."

"However did you find that out?" Toby asked, "I think you are entitled to boast now."

"It wasn't a case of finding out, it is the only logical explanation for that mysterious affair with the goat. You see, whereas the other three attempts on her life had all been invented for my benefit, on this occasion she actually staged one, and for a very deliberate and carefully thought out purpose."

"I hate to quibble," Robin said, "but have you forgotten that she did have a miscarriage as a direct result of that incident? You can't honestly expect us to believe that was staged?"

"No, but it had nothing to do with the goat, it was just that the plan went wrong. I imagine that in this case Cath got it right when she said that Lizzie became over-excited and wriggled about, so that Anne did indeed drop her, instead of merely having to pretend she had done so. Dropped her, moreover, on the wrong side of the fence, which must have given her the fright of her life and probably caused all the trouble later. Nevertheless, at the time, she was still inwardly composed and determined enough to push through the rest of her plan."

"Namely, as they say . . . ?"

"You may recall that when Jane described what happened next, she mentioned that Anne demanded to be allowed to lie down, but, the sofa being too cramped for the purpose, she was taken upstairs so that she could stretch out comfortably. All of which, of course, was according to the script; to arrange matters in such a way as to be alone in Cath's bedroom, drop the pill into the bottle of sleeping tablets, give it a good shake and then close her eyes and wait for Harry to come and fetch her home. She must have been delighted with herself too, because the lovely thing was that if the poison got to Mary by mistake, it would have suited her purpose just as well. Which is exactly what did happen, only she never had the satisfaction of knowing it, poor dear."

"Very clever!" Toby said, "I congratulate you! I can't imagine how or where Anne got hold of her knockout drop, but I am not so silly as to believe you have overlooked a little point like that."

"No, and as a matter of fact, Toby, it is entirely due to you that the information came my way."

"Well, that's good news. One does sometimes get a little tired of playing the passive role. Tell me, though, how did I do it?"

"By chickening out of the funeral. If you had come with me, I should not have driven Anne's father to London and I should not have had my interesting and informative conversation with Miles Stevenson."

"Oh, I see! After all, the role does seem to have been more passive than I had hoped, but heigh ho for that! Did Miles tell you where she got the cyanide?"

"Not in so many words, but it amounted to that. One of the interesting facts he let slip was that he'd used up his home leave for this year, which in effect meant that he'd been in England quite recently."

"Oh, well done! I can see what a big step forward that was!"

"You're right, because he'd already told he was a doctor; and a doctor, mark you, working far away on the Persian Gulf. None of your poison books and National Health watchdogs to trip you up there! Another interesting remark he made was that Anne had not needed to choose that way to kill herself because she had other means to hand, and when I queried this he replied very firmly that he knew it for a fact. To cap it all, he ended by saying that Anne worried too much and often quite unnecessarily. Well, we were all agreed on that, but Miles related it specifically to her father, and he described him as being much more stoical than she realised. Significant, don't you think, when you add it all together?"

"Most!" Toby agreed, "you won't catch me lagging behind."

"So, you see, neither Tom, nor Cath, nor Jane, nor any combination of the three invented that story about seeing her in earnest and intimate conversation with the young man in the restaurant. The mistake was in interpreting it as a love affair, or, as in Cath's way-out version, as a plot to create a little baby son for Harry. What they were actually discussing, without a doubt, was Mr Monk's illness, and Anne was using all her wiles and playing on all his finer feelings to get Miles to supply her with a lethal dose, for purposes of euthanasia, in the event of her father's pain and distress becoming unbearable."

"He must have had some very fine feelings indeed to have agreed to that!" Toby remarked.

"Oh, he had; the finest there are. He was hopelessly and passionately in love with her and had been for years."

"And confessed as much to someone he had known for less than a couple of hours?"

"No, but he virtually admitted that he had gone to the Middle East because his heart was broken. And why else would he have dropped everything to travel thousands of miles at his own expense for the funeral of someone he wasn't even related to? Just to keep his godfather company? The idea is absurd! No, mine has to be the answer and if you can give me a better one you both win a gold medal and a bottle of champagne."

Neither of them was disposed to take me up on it, then or later, although I suspect that Toby, who is not very romantic, still cudgels his brains from time to time.

Poor Jane did not survive to enjoy married life with Harry. On the eve of their wedding, when Tom was driving her home from a late and lavish party, he cornered too fast on a winding lane, lost control of the steering and crashed straight through somebody's gate and into their front door. No one in the house was injured, but he and Jane were killed instantly.

I never discovered the full truth about their relationship, but not long ago Mrs Nicholson shed a shaft of light on it when she told me that Jane had been strongly attracted to Harry ever since the family moved into Hollings Farm, hinting that she had rushed into her unsuitable marriage in a fit of pique at his choosing Anne instead. So perhaps she and Tom were two of a kind, both on the make and both prepared to back the other's cause in order to further their own.

Soon afterwards, Cath moved into the big house, which looks tidier these days, although the cuisine is a lot less haute than it used to be. Mrs Chalmers seems pleased with the arrangement and of course Cath is in her element, but I fear her days are numbered. During the past six months she has seen off a good few Nannies and au pair girls of varying degrees of sluttishness, uppishness and incompetence, but she seems powerless to oust Harry's latest acquisition, a stern and beautiful young Scandinavian, named Inge.

I met her for the second time when I was staying with Toby last weekend. She was standing, rapt and motionless, at the top of Platt's Meadow, with Lizzie, promoted now to a push chair, at her side and the horses and donkey grouped round her at a respectful distance.

I concluded that she was admiring the view, but this was not so, for after we had remarked on it in a desultory way she fell into a reflective silence, which ended with her announcing in her most disapproving tone that she did not care to see so much good land going to waste and that in her country it would be used to provide homes for the people.

I feel sure Harry is right when he says that Lizzie understands everything, for she rolled up her eyes and then very deliberately seized the doll which Anne had given her on her second birthday and tossed it on to the ground.